Reign of the Brute

A Brute Story

~

A novel by
Matthew H. Jones

Also by Matthew H. Jones

Reign of the Brute

A Brute Story

For GJ and JR, always

'…the human face as glimpsed in the street had been one of the keenest torments he had been forced to endure.'
– Yoris-Karl Huysmans, *A Rebours*

CHAPTER 1

At long last, life was worth living. Years of debt, poverty and struggle were behind me. I had no job, nor any need for one. I'd developed a mild alcohol dependence and was happier than I'd ever been.

I was now a landlord, meaning I profited handsomely from the common need for shelter. My first question to prospective tenants was *why don't you buy a home of your own?* - a reasonable query usually met with ingracious jabbering about housing costs. I'd then calmly explain that all it took was good sense and hard work, after all, *I'd* managed to ascend the property ladder with little more than some initiative and a resourceful head on my shoulders. Most tenants weren't receptive to such advice however, instead boring me with details of the supposed housing crisis.

I'd secured my first property, a pristine, split-level dockside apartment, after successfully blackmailing my former employer (a large supermarket chain) for £600k+ and buying the place outright. It was a bright, capacious duplex decorated to a tastefully minimal standard and lit by brushed, elegant uplights. The balcony overlooked the harbour and the lobby was guarded by a submissive manservant who addressed me with the requisite level of awe.

My housing fortune negated the need for work (cruel,

hateful work) and I spent the majority of my days padding languidly about the rooms, nibbling salmon and sipping rambunctious Chardonnay. It was a bountiful time, worlds beyond the debilitating poverty of my previous existence, a demeaning grind wherein I bathed in a fishtank and subsisted on soggy luncheon meat.

I'd been assisted in the acquisition by Sheena, an ex-muckraker with whom I now cohabited. It was by no means a romantic relationship (we'd never shared an attraction) but instead one of co-dependent triumph: a shared realisation that it was both possible and honourable to extort money if one genuinely deserved it.

She'd also been employed by the supermarket, and despite our good fortune, had kept her job, somewhat bafflingly insisting that she now enjoyed the work. Supposedly the notion of working for 'fun' rather than financial necessity gave her a rush of power and superiority over her halfwitted colleagues. Happily, she also brought home a monthly wage, a modest but welcome sum that covered our essentials: hare legs, Beaujolais, and all the onion powder we could eat.

This all changed when she initiated the purchase of a second property. It was to be a buy-to let investment that'd provide us a comfortable income and enable her to leave her job, for who'd work like a dog when they could comfortably exploit the desperate?

She'd acquired the mortgage by releasing a sizeable chunk of equity on our apartment and taking advantage of the current interest rate, which had apparently risen or fallen, though I didn't know which.

Breezing through the application process we'd found ourselves in the enviable position of househunting for somewhere in which we'd never live, meaning our list of prerequisites was hilariously small. No toilet? Get a bucket. No running water? Stand out in the rain. Defective heating? Put a jumper on.

Given we'd not be occupying it ourselves, we opted for

a tumbledown shitheap on the Bullmarsh Estate: a three-room slum on the verge of collapse, saturated with black mould and infested with cockroaches and dead cats.

The windows were so poorly fitted that condensation ran down the walls and caused green shoots to sprout from the carpet, a quirk we'd later market as an indoor garden feature. Additionally the oven, refrigerator and radiators were knackered, rusted and stinking, while the boiler gurgled and clanked like a medieval torture device.

Despite the appalling conditions our lettings agent, a moisturised dreamboat named Stu, had guaranteed us two thousand pounds a month in rent, reasoning that *someone* would pay it. 'People are desperate.' he said, shooting us a wink that caused me an involuntary erection.

Having not rented for a year or more, I'd conditioned myself to forget my past and assume the role of a proud, entitled homeowner. I often browsed estate agents' windows, snorting at the grimy kennels they passed off as homes, inordinately pleased at my own good fortune. Was it possible I'd succeeded simply because I was cleverer than most people? Surely if they had the foresight to blackmail their employers, they too could snap up a smart city apartment with underfloor heating and quartz work surfaces.

As promised, Stu had dozens of applicants, all willing to live in debilitating squalor if it meant a roof over their heads. Several of them even expressed excitement at the prospect of making it 'homely', to which I countered that even the tiniest pinhole in a wall would incur crippling deposit deductions. The same applied for any traces of wear and tear, chipped paintwork, burn marks, stains, even a misplaced fridge magnet.

Eventually Stu called us into his office with news. He'd had an enquiry from 'Ed', a moneyed, childless twit who worked as a designer of some sort. 'He's on a very good wage,' said Stu, explaining the lucrative nature of graphic and 3D design. I didn't listen, instead gazing at his payslips and wondering if we could nudge up his monthly rent payments.

'Could we add a few hundred to his rent?' said Sheena, thinking exactly the same thing.

Stu smiled. 'Of course we can,' he said, as reassuring as a grandparent. 'A bit extra won't hurt.'

While not much to a high earner like Ed, several hundred pounds a month could feasibly afford us a hatchback or a minibreak to Broadstairs. Ultimately it was his civic duty to pay over the odds, for how else would we broaden our horizons?

'I'll give him a call,' said Stu, his bicep tensed beneath his shirtsleeves.

CHAPTER 2

We'd requested a meeting with Ed before permitting him to spend a small fortune renting our shithole.

We were sitting in Muggins Cafe, a horrible rat's nest decorated with portraits of insects and Klansmen. The proprietor's beard was peppered with lice and it was rumoured he kept his wife prisoner in the cellar. (Supposedly on quiet days you could hear her screaming over the tinkling of spoons and crockery.)

'We've got to make sure this guy's not weird,' said Sheena, sipping Chardonnay at nine in the morning. 'I don't want a weirdo.'

We were eating cow meat and leafing through Ed's paperwork. 'What's a digital conceptualiser?' I said.

'It's to do with computers,' said Sheena, clearly totally clueless. 'Everyone works with computers these days.' She mumbled something about modems and refilled her glass with a shaky hand.

The cafe door chimed open and a man walked in. Was that Ed? I hoped not, for his appearance immediately filled me with hatred and disgust. He was in his early thirties, with glasses and a sparse little beard. His hair was wispy and thin and he had legs like a clawfoot bath. Given we were the only customers he approached us hesitantly.

'Er, I'm Ed?' he said. 'I'm here about the, er - flat, I

suppose.'

Despite my position of power he made me feel stupid and small. Why? He was wearing a *backpack* for God's sake. By rights he should've been begging for my approval.

'Are you getting a drink?' said Sheena, deliberately not ordering him one. (Stu had advised we treat all prospective tenants like dirt).

'Er...okay?' he said.

He went to the counter and I wanted very much to jab a knife into his eye.

'What do you think?' said Sheena.

'I hate him.' I said.

'Me too.'

He reappeared with a coffee and sat down. He stirred in a sachet of sugar and said nothing. We watched him intently.

'So...okay?' he said. *Was that a question?*

'Okay.' I said, feeling like an idiot.

Thankfully Sheena jumped in. 'So, *Ed*,' she said. 'Is that short for Edward?'

Ed looked at us from behind his horn rims. 'What do you think?' he said, wildly infuriating.

Sheena continued, admirably unflustered: 'we just wanted to meet you, make sure you're suitable, that kind of thing. You can't be too careful, you see.'

Ed pondered this and rolled his eyes. 'O-*kay* then.' he said, eliciting in me an overwhelming urge to hit him in the face.

This discourse continued for half an hour, a strained exercise as we tried to extract the information we required. Eventually we relented and offered him the flat, reasoning it'd be easier to rent to someone we hated.

Once the agreements had been made, he rose and put on his backpack. 'Thanks, I guess,' he said, totally ungrateful. Was he *trying* to anger us? He stalked out of the cafe and hopefully into the path of an oncoming car.

The cafe owner reappeared at our table. 'More wine?'

he said, clearing Sheena's empties. 'I could take you down to the cellar if you like - pick a nice bottle?'

Wary of unlawful imprisonment, Sheena declined and paid for the breakfast. He thanked us and gave us a bag of cow meat scraps. 'Come back soon my friends.' he said, filling a dog bowl for his wife.

CHAPTER 3

Ed was scheduled to move in on a Saturday, a privilege Stu charged him through the nose for. We made no effort to clean the flat, reasoning it'd be a character-building experience for him. Might he produce a documentary about urban survival techniques?

As part of his tenancy agreement he'd requested a bed, as if he were a nobleman or Persian prince. Naturally we'd ignored his demands, instead providing a sodden mattress Sheena had found in a skip. 'It's not fucking Windsor Castle.' she'd said.

He'd also requested the fridge be repaired, presumably so he could chill his lobster tails and Wagyu steak cuts.

'Does he think we're millionaires?' I said, balking at the cost of refrigerator maintenance. *That's money that could buy me a new casserole pot*, I thought.

'Don't worry,' said Sheena. 'We'll get him a bucket of ice. Does the same job'

'Good thinking,' I said. 'In a way it's more convenient. Takes up less space.'

Leafing through the contract, I couldn't believe his list of demands. It read like the dressing room requirements of a millionaire rock band. In addition to the bed and the fridge, he wanted the hole in the ceiling fixed, the gas leak repaired, and the dead birds removed from the bathroom sink. What next? Truffles on a platter of gold? I was legitimately concerned we'd onboarded a problem tenant. My only comfort was the thousands of pounds we'd receive in rent each month, easily covering the mortgage and leaving me enough for pricey masturbation subscriptions.

We'd be better off than we'd ever been and all I could think about were ways to make more. Sheena assured me this was perfectly normal and was simply how capitalism worked.

'How do you think Superdrug got so big?' she said, not unreasonably.

~

We visited the property the day before Ed was due to move in. It was located on the Bullmarsh estate, boxed in among a pile-up of grey block houses. The estate was under threat of demolition from the local council, eager to cleanse the area of 'scum' – as one MP put it – and sell the land to a resourceful property developer.

Inside it smelt like a washing machine full of sewage. There was mould throughout: furry, sodden patches that darkened every corner like bruises on a banana, none of which we'd address because it posed no medical threat whatsoever.

'That'll come off with a sponge,' said Sheena, gasping into an asthma inhaler.

The wallpaper was soaked and slipping off the plaster like slow-cooked lamb, revealing brickwork gummy with residual wallpaper paste.

'Just needs a few drawing pins,' said Sheena.

Stu was already there, doing press-ups in the living room and listening to an audiobook called *Silencing the Maggots: Arguments for Cruelty in Management.*

'Oh hey guys,' he said, his skin shimmering with sweat. 'All ready for your new tenant? He's made a few requests to get the place cleaned up -'

Sheena waved a dismissive hand. 'Forget all that,' she said. 'He'll get what he's given. We're here to make sure he doesn't pinch anything. Greedy little rat.'

We bent to Ed's demands just once, by begrudgingly tossing the dead birds from the bathroom sink out of the window. They landed with a *poof* on the pavement outside and were immediately mauled by children hunting for roadkill.

'A good little dinner, that,' said Sheena, watching the birds being torn apart. 'Lucky kids. When I was that age I was happy if I got a bucket of mud for my tea.'

Sheena's upbringing had been a spartan grind through the harshest backwaters of South Wales, an experience she claimed had inflicted on her incurable trenchfoot. She'd ended up in Cardiff, manufacturing sausage casings and contemplating suicide, when her supervisor mentioned his daughter's philosophy degree. 'He said it was three years of sad contemplation,' she recalled. 'It sounded perfect.'

Despite never actually killing herself, she'd come close before our blackmail plot had bore fruit, even managing to procure the high-grade arsenic required to finish the job. In a strange way I'd been supportive of her decision, for how else does one escape the modern day rent trap?

Such lows were unthinkable now, as she shuttled from room to room, whittling Ed's home comforts down to nothing. We'd not bothered fixing the gas leak, preferring instead to charge him for the damage and claiming he'd smashed the boiler in anger. Similarly, we'd agreed to ignore the hole in the ceiling, pretending it was a superficial crack until Ed moved in and exacerbated it with unreasonable door banging.

'All looks good to me,' said Sheena, drawing deeply on the inhaler as the mould devastated her lungs.

'Great stuff,' said Stu. 'I'm sure he'll love it here.'

~

We arrived home and poured two massive gins.

'I hope he doesn't cause trouble,' said Sheena, studying Ed's contract. 'Especially after we made the place so nice for him.'

'He should be grateful,' I said. 'Some people don't understand the pressures of being a landlord.'

'You're right,' she said. 'It's a hard job.'

She was right - it *was* a hard job. We'd not even started being landlords and already we'd spent nearly *three hours* on forms, contracts, insurance, etc. I hoped once Ed had moved in we could relax and concentrate on banking our money.

I'd read somewhere that tenants spend over half their income on rent, and why not? Besides Plum Duff and football stickers, what else was there to spend your money on? Even if I engaged a full-time prostitute and drank myself half to death I'd *still* likely struggle to spend all the cash we'd collect from Ed, so God knows what he might've wasted it on.

Sheena poured more gin and lit a Thrushman's cigarette. 'Do you think we should repaint the kitchen?' she said idly.

I thought about it. Debating colour swatches would fill at least an afternoon, if not a whole day. It was a yes from me.

'Actually, don't worry about it,' she said, easing into a snooze. 'I'm sure it's fine.'

If we'd had any sense we would've relished this period of inactivity. We genuinely had nothing in our lives more pressing than a passing discontent at our soft furnishings. It was not to last.

CHAPTER 4

The next morning the phone rang before I'd had a chance to expel any sperm.

'Who the *fuck* phones this early?' screamed Sheena. Her bedroom door was closed but I heard a *smash* as she hurled her morning whisky at the wall.

'Hello?' I said.

'Hey, it's me.' said Stu.

'Morning,' I said, fumbling with a particularly stubborn boner.

'Got a bit of a problem,' he said. 'With Ed.'

Christ, I thought. *One day and already he's causing problems.*

'Tell him to drop dead.' I said.

'I wish I could,' said Stu. 'But he wants to talk to you. Apparently the flat's not up to standard.'

What on earth did he mean? Granted, the place had the odd cobweb but otherwise it was delightful.

'Can you get over there this morning?' he said.

'Can't you go instead?' I said. 'We're repainting the kitchen.'

'I offered. He's adamant he wants to see you.'

'Fine,' I said. 'But is there a way we can charge him for this? A call-out fee or something?'

'Way ahead of you,' said Stu. 'I've added it to his fees. I thought three hundred should cover it.'

'Okay then,' I said. 'I'll book a taxi.' I replaced the receiver and noticed my boner hadn't subsided.

~

Sheena had refused to accompany me, explaining how she'd not be dragged from her bed by a bespectacled media twonk. 'I'd end up giving him a slap,' she said.

Ignoring the taxi driver's incessant racism (he thought police officers should be allowed to kill five immigrants a day), I thought instead about Sheena's near-constant drinking. I admired her greatly for her fortitude, wishing I had the stamina to drink myself senseless every day.

During our initial few months together we'd had some enviable benders, once enjoying a shot of ouzo every five minutes for nearly three hours, an exercise that'd left me partially blind and vomiting onto a neighbour's cat.

'It just makes sense,' the driver continued, convinced he'd make a great foreign secretary. 'You won't get no more crime, that's for bloody sure.'

His rampant prejudice ensured he wasn't tipped, instead I spat on his car as he drove away, neatly dousing his Britain First sticker in phlegm. I dearly hoped he'd soon be killed in an accident, an upturn in fortune that'd sadden precisely no one.

There were suitcases and boxes in the front garden, evidence of Ed's imminent takeover of my property portfolio. I felt strangely possessive as I envisaged him wandering around inside, littering the place with junk and personal effects. As a preventative measure I'd tell him to keep clutter to an absolute minimum and steal anything I thought he mightn't miss.

I let myself in because it was my flat, and immediately smelt vape smoke. *You're disgusting*, I thought. Why couldn't he smoke real cigs like Sheena? With little else to do, she often smoked a hundred a day, most nights smoking herself to sleep. The vape smelled like figs and bin water:

sweet but weirdly rotten, like a Hawaiian pizza or putrefied corpse.

'Ed,' I called, as sternly as I could. 'There's no smoking in here. This is coming out of your deposit.'

I reached the living room and saw him sitting on a cushioned stool staring at a laptop. He was sucking at the vape like a freshly birthed piglet.

'Oh, er, hi?' he said, not turning around. Was he watching pornography?

'What's the problem, Ed?' I said. 'Stu said you wanted to see me.'

'Er, okay,' he said. 'I guess I did.'

Why did he make me so uncomfortable? Surely I was his superior in every way imaginable?

He tapped a few laptop keys before snapping the lid shut, an aggressive, purposeful gesture that caused me to tense like a MP. He looked at me and I noticed his beard had thickened since I'd last seen him, while his jaw seemed broader and fleshier. Alarmingly he was also now wearing a vest, though not the type worn for wifebeating, more the type I imagined gym enthusiasts might wear when deciding who to rape in a sports bar.

He arose and was taller than I remembered, something I also found intimidating.

'So, erm,' he said, puckering his lips. Was he going to kiss me? 'I wanted to go over a couple of things.'

'Oh fine,' I said. 'What's the matter? Is anything wrong?'

He led me around the flat, pointing out every little niggle and moaning about how it should've been fixed before the moving date. I told him there was a skirting board shortage and that we'd resolve it all immediately, both complete lies. *You can rot in this dump*, I thought.

This seemed to placate him and he stopped mithering, even going so far as to offer me a rice cake.

'No thanks,' I said, with as little warmth as possible. 'I've got to go.' *Choke on your rice cake,* I thought, booking a taxi home.

CHAPTER 5

Very quickly Ed became a problem. We were now contacted by Stu on a weekly basis, asking when we'd provide a serviceable bed (apparently the mattress had once been a flies nest and maggots were now appearing by the handful), and when the hole in the ceiling would be repaired.

'Tell him it's a skylight,' said Sheena, dismissing Ed's concerns as infantile entitlement. It was 1pm and she was hooting drunk, having had five whiskies for breakfast and only a cocktail sausage for sustenance. 'Most people would kill for that kind of luxury.'

I relayed the message to Stu and hung up the phone. 'Stu's going to tell him,' I said. 'Hopefully that'll keep him off our backs for a while.'

Sheena lit a Thrushman's and tottered off for more drink. We'd recently bought a new fridge, one with humidity control and a plumbed ice dispenser, meaning our booze remained frosty and wonderfully chilled. Stu suggested donating the old one to Ed but I'd vetoed the idea, concerned he might think us a charity.

'If he wants a fridge he can buy a fucking fridge,' said Sheena, killing the discussion stone dead.

This dialogue continued for several weeks, as Ed relentlessly pestered us to transform the flat into a

Venetian penthouse. On top of the roof and the fridge, apparently now the boiler wasn't good enough because it didn't produce hot water.

'What does he want?' said Sheena. 'A thermal spring? Tell him to piss off to Iceland.'

We parried his demands a while longer, ducking his calls and advising Stu charge him for his unsolicited requests. This, however, soon came to an abrupt halt.

~

We were called into the estate agents' office and ushered into a back room reserved for important clients.

'Can I get you anything?' said Brynn, a servile snake who was ascending the ladder of estate agency with a view to becoming truly evil. 'Tea, coffee...'

'Cava,' said Sheena. 'Two bottles.'

He mumbled something about an entertainment surcharge but she waved him away. 'Just do it,' she said, crumpling her empty can of gin and mixer. 'Can't you see I'm parched?'

He slunk off to make some enquiries and we idly tore posters off the walls and scratched the table with keys.

'Do you think estate agents feel love?' I said.

'Of course not,' said Sheena, stamping cigarette ash into the carpet. 'Estate agents are Satan's representatives on earth.'

Stu appeared at the door with two bottles of fizz. 'Sorry about Brynn,' he said. 'He's new. I've told him about our arrangement.'

Sheena tutted. 'I don't want him talking to us anymore.'

'Consider it done,' said Stu, his teeth causing me snow blindness.

We uncorked a bottle and poured out the nourishing slosh. I'd had an escalope for breakfast and the bubbles tickled my senses immediately.

This had become routine during our visits to the estate

agent. We'd already bought two properties, earned them a hefty percentage, and hinted heavily at buying a third. As a result, Stu remained appropriately deferent towards us, an obvious ploy to retain our business and secure another commission. Might he offer me a handjob to lock in our business?

'So what's the problem?' said Sheena, finishing the first bottle without ceremony. 'Why are we here?'

Stu took a breath and folded his arms. 'It's Ed.' he said.

She shook her head, infuriated.

Stu took a breath. 'He says he's going to stop paying the rent.'

Sheena snatched the empty bottle from the table and hurled it at the wall, carpeting the floor in glass.

In an instant I foresaw my life tumbling down around me. Ed's rent was our sole source of income, a hard-earned monthly bung enabling us to wallow in lamb's lettuce and gin cocktails till the sun came up. Without it I was concerned Sheena would have to work *full-time* – a culture shock that'd surely lead her back towards suicide. It also meant I'd need to downgrade the quality of my salmon ration, something I was absolutely unprepared to do.

'No,' I stuttered. 'He can't do that. We need our money.'

Stu showed us an email from Ed. Apparently he'd grassed us up to the Environmental Health Department and was now withholding rent under warrant of habitability. 'It means it's not a habitable residence.' said Stu helpfully.

'What kind of rule is that?' said Sheena, gouging at the table with a shard of glass. 'People used to live in *caves*, for God's sake! Are *they* habitable?'

Stu shook his head gingerly. 'No -' he ventured. *Was she serious?*

'And what about during the war? People lived in *trenches*.'

'Sheena's right,' I said. 'Compared to the war it's a lovely flat.'

Stu exhaled and rolled his eyes. 'Yes, yes it is,' he said. 'But under today's guidelines you need to make the place habitable, and that means no gas leaks, no holes in the ceiling, a working refrigerator -'

'We gave him a bucket of ice,' said Sheena, banging her fist on the table. 'Do you think that came cheap?'

In fact it *had* come cheap: we'd found the bucket in a tree and the ice was scraped from the back of an old chest freezer.

'No, no, of course not,' said Stu, cracking his knuckles. 'I know you put a lot of work into making it nice.' He tried to smile. 'However, government guidelines state that some of these niggles need to be, you know, *ironed out* before the tenant moves in.'

'Okay, okay,' I said, trying to calm Sheena's juddering face. 'So all we need to do to get our money back is fix a few things. That shouldn't be too difficult, should it?'

Stu shook his head. 'Absolutely not. There are always ways of fixing things without breaking the bank. I can recommend a couple of handymen that aren't too...*discerning*, if you know what I mean.'

Sheena had cracked the second bottle of cava and glugged despondently, clearly furious at having to spend a single penny on Ed's upkeep. 'He already lives like a king,' she said. 'What more does he want?'

Stu agreed to put us in touch with some cowboy tradesmen who'd fudge the job enough to pass the government's draconian safety checks. 'They're cheap,' he said. 'Very cheap.'

Sheena later collapsed on the living room floor, catatonic after skulling a bottle of windscreen wiper fluid in the taxi home. Sitting alone, I looked around our beautiful apartment and winced at the thought of her having to go back to work. How would she drink herself blind in the middle of the day if she had to hold down a job? The service sector didn't generally condone such behaviour, while office managers routinely humiliated their staff by restricting their drinking to non-lethal levels. Perhaps she could become an airline pilot or political lobbyist? I made a vague promise to get her the application forms tomorrow.

I fried a pork knuckle and fell asleep with an anxious brain. We needed to fix the flat. We needed our money.

CHAPTER 6

I was considering Stu's shortlist of tradesmen and wondering which of them might offer the least blatant swindle. I assumed they were all illegitimate conmen and expected very little in terms of craftsmanship, hoping instead they'd take a clawhammer to Ed's skull.

My last contact with a tradesmen had been several years ago, when I'd tussled with a gruff, toothless handyman who operated out of a tumbledown sex shed. He'd been missing since being driven off a bridge, the police investigation into which was now closed, safely presuming him dead.

I telephoned the first thug on the list and he answered with heavy, growling breaths. Clearly he was masturbating and immediately made me feel uncomfortable.

'Talk to meee,' he snarled, his voice croaky from a diet of fags and dog food.

'Hi there,' I said. 'I got your number from Stu. He said you'd be able to fix our flat.'

'I'll fix you,' he said, absolutely terrifying. I could hear the claggy slime licking around his mouth as he spoke.

'Okay thanks, bye.' I said, hurriedly hanging up the phone.

I struck his name from the list and dialled the next one.

'*Please* stop calling,' came the voice. It sounded devastated. 'I've told you, no more surgery. I've done my bit. I'm out.'

'Sorry,' I said. 'Have I got the wrong number? Are you a tradesman?'

He went silent.

'Hello?' I said. 'Are you okay?'

I heard a faint, whimpering sound. Was he crying?

'I'm in pain,' he said. '*So* much pain.'

'Crumbs,' I said. 'Have you tried Nurofen?'

'You wouldn't believe what they did to me.'

I sighed, wondering why any of this was my problem. 'Could you fix my flat?' I said. 'It's got a hole in the ceiling.'

'Help...me...' he said, utterly desperate. 'Help meeee.'

I hung up the phone. *Help yourself, tradesman.* I thought.

I dialled the last name on the list. It rang repeatedly but with no answer. I left a message outlining our requests but expected nothing back; I assumed it was a burner phone used by the tradesman to traffick vagrants into his lumberyard. *Thanks for nothing, Stu,* I thought. Would we have to use safety-registered workmen now?

I poured a gin and decamped to the balcony to throw pebbles at the doorman. Sheena was unconscious in a lounge chair, a dwindling Thrushman's trailing ash from her mouth. Interestingly, she only had one lung, the result of a botched medical procedure that left her prone to asthma and shortness of breath. It was part of the reason she drank so much: being blackout drunk meant she didn't wake in the middle of the night wheezing and gasping for breath. Her skin was scarred puce and I could hear her chest rasping as she tumbled through unconsciousness, oblivious after drinking a litre of vodka.

It was then that the phone rang. Ed again? What did he want now? Diamanté candelabras?

'Hello?' I said.

'Who's that?' came the voice. I recognised it instantly.

It was the tradesman I'd known years earlier, the same tradesman who'd killed my roommate with a spanner and who'd been written off as dead by the investigating officers. His voice pricked me like a thorny jockstrap, returning memories of unscrupulous landlords and alcoholic policemen I'd tried so diligently to forget.

'Handyman,' I said. 'It's me.'

'Who gave you this number?' he said, his voice gravelled from cigs.

He was naturally intimidating, but my terror was heightened knowing how many people he'd killed. I faltered, envisaging him climbing out of the phone receiver and pulling my teeth out.

'Erm, er,' I stuttered like a faulty engine. 'Stu gave it to me. Do you know Stu?'

Handyman growled. 'Stu -' he said, sounding very much like he wanted to kill Stu. 'I know Stu.'

'Okay,' I said, treading lightly. 'So do you think you could fix our flat? I'm sure it wouldn't take long. You'd not even need to do a good job.'

'A botch job?' he said, his interest piqued.

'Yes,' I said. 'A botch job would be great. Could you do it anytime soon?'

He paused, breathing like a turbine. 'Give me a month,' he said. 'I'm away at the moment.'

I wondered where on earth he was. Employed in a migrant camp? I imagined him stalking the exercise yard, chuffing cigs and picking off escapees with a hunting rifle.

'That's fine.' I said.

I heard a sawing sound and assumed he was torturing someone. 'Got to go,' he said. 'See you in a month.'

I skulled my gin and sat back, spooked and oddly drained. Talking to Handyman had plunged me into a psychological netherworld of humiliation and powerlessness, a mindset I assumed I'd suppressed through my sustained period of heavy drinking. I guzzled the remainder of the gin bottle and watched a documentary celebrating music videos by sex offenders of the 70s.

~

The next month was gruelling. Without an income we'd been forced to delve into our savings, most of which were gobbled up by wine subscriptions and Sheena's weakness for cashmere. ('It feels like my uncle's back hair,' she said fondly.)

We'd eventually had a tense summit in the kitchen.

'That's the last bottle,' I said, pouring two half pints of gin. 'We're dry.'

'Right then,' said Sheena, half-drunk from lunchtime. 'We need money. What are our options?'

'It looks like you might have to go back to work,' I said. 'How do you feel about that?'

She lit a calming cig. 'Shouldn't be a problem,' she said. 'If it's only for a few weeks. Piece of piss.'

I was hugely relieved. I'd expected pushback from Sheena but it seemed she'd openly embraced the idea of enforced menial gruntwork.

'It'll get me out of the house,' she said. 'Might even make a few friends as well.'

Friends? I thought. Why did she need friends when she owned her own property?

'Great,' I said. 'Have you thought about where you might work?'

'There's a job going at Muggins cafe,' she said. 'Cleaning the meat scrapers and so on. Pay's not great but apparently you get a lot of free cow meat.'

'Sounds good,' I said. 'The more cow meat the better.'

'Only problem is drink,' she said. 'How much can you drink during a working day? Is there a limit?'

I recalled my previous job with horror. I'd been so dictatorially ruled over I'd not even been allowed a fourpack before my shift. This was patently ridiculous given it was a such a victimless crime, a harmless indiscretion noticeable only to the revolting general public.

'You can probably drink as much as you like,' I said, reassuring her. 'That's what most people do.'

She seemed happy at this, swigging her drink with the hardened charm of a hooligan ringleader. 'I'll go in tomorrow.' she said.

CHAPTER 7

Sheena was hired without question by the proprietor of Muggins - clearly he had plans to kidnap her but we didn't worry unnecessarily about that. Her official title was Fat Sluicer, a thankless role that involved scraping animal fat off various surfaces and depositing it in an industrial bin barrel. The coagulated residue would later be repurposed into candles for online craft sellers.

Returning home after her first day, she was so tired she fell asleep before she was able to drink the bottle of vodka she'd stolen from work. I covered her with a blanket and drank it myself, sharpened by its crystalline warmth.

Being nauseatingly wrecked and smoking mortal quantities of Thrushman's ensured our appetites remained conveniently suppressed and the necessity for food kept to a minimum. We had joyless foodstuffs stored away in the cupboards (sea snails, wort butter) but held off eating until it was absolutely necessary. Sheena subsisted on the cow meat she got from work, while I had no use for muscle energy given my dangerously sedentary lifestyle. Most days I awoke at midday and lay in bed staring at my scrotum. When this became tiresome I'd pull on a terrycloth gown and pad to the kitchen for gizzards and mustard fruit. I'd then stare at the telly until I felt sick, at which point Sheena would arise and stabilise herself with drink.

On sunny days we'd loaf on the balcony like caterpillars, leaf through homeware catalogues and debate cornicing. We'd smoke cigs with the breezy languor of recovering addicts while quaffing gin like distressed widows. Unfortunately, such idling stopped abruptly when Sheena secured the job at the cafe, whose opening hours meant she was often required to work as late as 4pm.

She was late for work every single day, gruellingly hungover and smelling like vegetable sweat. 'He doesn't care,' she said of the owner. 'He's addicted to worming tablets.'

Her cafe duties included spitting in customers' tea and feeding the owner's wife when her screams became too deafening. He forbade her from cooking anything, which he claimed was his job alone, as if frying dog food involved any kind of culinary prowess whatsoever.

She stole admirably from the place, often returning with plates, cutlery and customers' wallets, all lifted without a second thought. 'If I'm going to break my back I want something to show for it.' she said, quite fairly.

Tonight she'd only managed to thieve a bottle of rum but it was enough to knock me off balance and vomit in the kitchen sink. I blacked out and wondered if tomorrow would pan out any differently. I predicted it wouldn't.

~

Sheena's income afforded us a spartan lifestyle only mildly preferable to destitution. We ate very little, subsisting instead on Thrushman's cigs and turkey pellets, occasionally splurging on batter for the cow meat. Perversely it worked out well: our malnourishment naturally increased the potency of the alcohol, meaning our drink outlay was conveniently slashed.

It was during one such binge that the phone rang, requiring I rise from my stupor and feign cognizance. 'Hello?' I said, slurring and dim.

'It's me.' said Handyman. He sounded breathless. Had he been torturing cats?

'Oh hi.' I said.

'What's this job you need doing?' he said. 'Who d'you need killed?'

I paused. Could I ask him to kill Ed? No. We needed Ed's money too much. 'Just some repairs,' I said. 'Need to make our flat habitable.'

'Oh yeah,' he said. 'I remember. The botch job. Cheap and nasty.'

'Yes that's it,' I said. 'Can you do it soon?'

I heard the click of a lighter. Probably his thousandth cig of the day, I thought.

'That's fine,' he said. 'Where's the 'ouse? I'll get cracking in the morning.'

I gave him the address and said I'd meet him there to ensure things weren't finished to too high a standard. Sheena had insisted on paying the absolute minimal for the repairs, even if it meant exposed wiring, sodden plaster or splintery woodwork. As long as it was habitable we could keep taking Ed's money. She'd also suggested a rent increase to cover the shortfall we'd suffered as a result of his insubordination, something with which I wholeheartedly agreed.

'He needs to be punished,' she said. 'He needs to learn.'

Absolutely, I thought, furious that he'd swindled us out of precious wedge.

Stu buried the increase in a contractual clause unnoticeable to all but the most hawkeyed of solicitors. 'He'll never see it,' he said. 'But it's all legal.'

He poured three glasses of cava and we toasted our good work.

'Just pleased to help you out,' he said, his teeth like sweetcorn kernels.

~

I arrived at the flat the next day with a hangover and a sweaty neck. I'd only had twelve vodkas yet still my head thumped. I'd done nothing wrong yet it felt like I was being punished. Why?

I was also anxious about seeing Handyman again after several years. Would he kill me? Enslave me? I often dreamed of his dimly lit shed, its walls saturated yellow and creaking with torture implements. I vividly recalled the mattress in the corner, its leather straps frayed with teeth marks and fabric stained a gruesome brown.

It was to this shed that I'd brought the bodies of two men I'd hit with a car some years earlier, an accident I barely remembered due to my deep and savage intoxication. Despite their injuries one of them was still breathing and could've quite easily been revived, a point I bravely raised at the time. In the interests of cleanliness, however, Handyman requested I let him sort it out, advising I wait outside while he beat him out of his misery, a compassionate end he likened to putting a bolt through a cow's head.

The front door was open when I arrived and I hoped Ed had fallen victim to a home invasion burglary. Sadly it wasn't the case, as Handyman's shitheap of a van peeked out from the side of the building. I followed the stench of builders' tobacco through the hall and into the kitchen where he sat at the table with three cigs in his mouth. Interestingly, he was drinking a can of cider, anomalous given his usual poison was strong, debilitating lager.

'Oh, good morning,' I said, trying to remember that *I* was now the boss. 'Would you like a cup of tea?'

He stamped a cig out on the floor. 'No tea,' he said. 'What do you want done?'

It was then that Ed shuffled in, a coffee cup in his hand. 'Oh, er, hi,' he said. 'Getting the place fixed up? Wow, I'd never have guessed.'

I badly wanted to thump his face so his lenses shattered and his eyeballs were cut to ribbons by glass. Would

Handyman help me? Dad had once told me never to hit a man with glasses but I'd dismissed it as another of his lies, like when he'd told me the TV presenters of my youth weren't out to hurt me.

'Why don't you go and have a wank,' said Handyman. 'We're talking.'

Ed snorted, and was about to retort, when he caught Handyman's gaze, a stare of *absolute evil* that'd chill the pubes off a bodybuilder.

'O-*kay*,' he said, clearly shaken but eager to remain aloof. 'I'll be in my room.'

I relished his fear and hoped he'd dream about Handyman's compassionless black eyes, small and beady like a lobster's.

'Little shit,' said Handyman as Ed left the room.

He lit two more cigs and rose, taking a pencil from behind his ear. 'Right. Let's see what we can do.'

I led him around the flat, pointing out the problems and clarifying the expendable nature of Ed's possessions. 'Break whatever you like.' I said.

'Load of old shit.' he said, stubbing a cig out on Ed's laundry. I agreed, spitting in the basket for good measure.

I pointed him to the hole in the bathroom ceiling. It was a sticky, seaweed-green orifice spooling with black slime. It'd been caused by structural weaknesses and rampant mould and had, apparently, broken the previous owner's neck when it'd caved in.

'We need that patched up,' I said. 'Could you do it?'

He reached up and prodded the gelatinous ooze. 'Easy,' he said. 'I just need to know how cheap you want to go.'

He explained that he could simply staple a binbag to the ceiling, covering the hole and saving me a bundle in materials. 'It'd take five minutes,' he said. 'Cost you a tenner.'

I weighed up my options. Whilst my mission was to make the flat habitable, ten pounds *did* seem a lot just to keep Ed's wretched head dry.

'No, don't worry about it,' I said. 'We'll sort something else out.'

I led him to the other pressing issue, that of the leaking gas pipe. Ed, evidently a cloying busybody, had isolated the source of the leak: a knackered plug valve beneath the kitchen boiler.

'That's going to need replacing,' said Handyman, wisely extinguishing his cig. 'That'll be a couple of 'undred quid, at least.'

I groaned, exhausted by Ed's demands. 'Is there any way you could do it for less?' I said. 'Ten, maybe twenty pounds at a push?'

He thumped the boiler and caused it to clank. 'Leave it to me,' he said.

He wolfed another cider and we read further down the list. He'd requested a refrigerator, as if he were a crown prince or rap superstar. Happily, Handyman knew an organ harvester who needed to offload a freezer that'd been used to store contaminated livers, and who'd donate it for a small fee.

'Done.' I said. 'Get it in as soon as possible.'

He scrawled this down in a notepad.

'Also, don't bother cleaning it,' I said. 'He's not a baby.'

'Anything else?' said Handyman, lighting more cigs.

'He also wants a bed,' I said. 'Apparently a mattress isn't enough.'

'I've got a mattress,' said Handyman. 'Would two mattresses count as a bed?'

'I'm sure they would.' I said, recalling his bloodstained torture bunk (good luck sleeping on *that*, Ed) 'It'd probably be twice as comfortable.'

He sucked his cigs and scrawled in his book. It fascinated me that he could read and write. Where might he have learnt such skills? The Screwfix catalogue?

'I'll bring it over.' he said.

He offered me a cider and we toasted our frugality. I even accepted his offer of a tradesman's' cig, a filterless death stick that smelt like burning compost. I spluttered like a faulty generator. Was his throat made of steel?

'Never normally share 'em,' he said. 'But I've 'ad to cut down. Doctor says me lungs are like cow stomachs.'

I choked down another lungful and felt it sizzling away layers of my oesophagus. It made a drag on a Thrushman's (routinely condemned as the deadliest brand in the world) feel like a tender bronchial massage.

'How many of these do you smoke a day?' I said. 'Now that you've cut down?'

He lit another one. 'Only an 'undred these days.' he said. 'Bloody doctors.'

I left him cursing and wheezing in the kitchen and ordered a taxi home. I was satisfied. Our work was done.

CHAPTER 8

Despite it being midday the flat was dark when I returned. Sheena was at work so I made a cup of tea and slipped in a vodka miniature. I opened her computer and checked the bank account, eagerly hoping to see some return to fortune. Inevitably, I was disappointed. I'd expected a same-day balance transfer from Ed (plus fees) for the missed rent he owed, now hopelessly overdue given the lengths we'd gone to sate his kingly needs. Maybe there'd been a hold-up with the bank, I thought, a common occurrence after they'd sold customers' data for bailout capital.

The day passed much like any other: I boiled an egg and threw it at the doorman, Sheena returned with her looted booze (Cypriot gorse wine tonight) and we drank it over a dinner of sugared chicken backs.

'Money in yet?' she said, her mouth like potted sausage.

'Not yet,' I said. 'I'm worried he'll wait until Handyman's finished.'

'But that could take *days*. How much longer am I supposed to keep working at that shithole?'

'I thought you said you liked it there.' I said (she'd said nothing of the sort).

'I *hate* it. Have you ever tried working in a cafe? It's revolting. Stinking powdered egg up your nose and bacon rind under your fingernails.'

Her fingertips *did* always look bulgy but I assumed that was fluid retention brought about by fervent alcoholism.

'The customers are disgusting as well. All builders with leathery mouths and clothes stinking of vinegar. *And* I have to feed that bloody woman in the cellar three times a day.' She screwed up her nose. 'And mop up her piss.'

That's awful, I said, sort-of sincerely.

'So he'd better start paying,' she said. 'Otherwise we're evicting him quicker than a pornstar's fart.'

~

Stu confirmed my fears on the phone the next day: Ed was refusing to pay a penny until Handyman had completed everything on the list, though it seemed he was unaware of the standard to which they'd be finished.

'He's expecting a Parisian chateau,' said Stu. 'Double bed, the works.'

I laughed heartily, imagining Ed's first glimpse of the death mattress.

'But remember,' he said, suddenly stern. 'It needs to be liveable. Keep in mind the warrant of habitability. I can keep hitting him with fees but if it's not habitable we're going to have a problem. He could request a health and safety assessment from the council.'

I was certain the council mustn't become involved, lest they fine us for turning on a tap or something equally ludicrous.

I explained the binbag and the mattress and quoted vaguely from the research I'd done on landlords' duty of care (lots of 'usuallys' and 'generallys'), assuring him that Handyman could be trusted to get the job done, be it murder or gas maintenance.

'Just make sure he's not got a leg to stand on,' said Stu. 'I want you guys to get what you deserve. You've worked so hard for this.' He was extraordinarily believable, like a celebrity claiming their child porn stash was actually book research. 'And once he's back on side, we can nudge up his rent payments. Call it admin for all the extra work.'

I agreed wholeheartedly. We *had* worked so hard for this. We'd suffered the indignity of renting for years and years, never knowing when or how we might procure a residence of our own. Thankfully housing poverty and human desperation had helixed into a solution that'd enabled us to circumvent the black dungeons of credit scoring and pay for a flat outright. Interestingly, we'd not once been asked how we'd been able to afford such an extravagance, instead we'd been lavished with peaches and wine hampers as reward for the time we'd invested in buying a house.

I phoned Handyman. 'Ed's refusing to pay until the work's done,' I said. 'Do you know when you'll be finished?'

I could hear shuffling and grunts down the phone, like something being dragged and restrained. 'Be with you in a sec,' he said. 'Just finishing something off.' Then came the rusty scrape of bolt cutters and maniacal screaming. Then sobs, silenced with a sharp *crack*. 'Alright,' he said, panting but strangely exuberant. 'What d'you want?'

'Is this a bad time?' I said, unsettled by the shallow breathing in the background.

'Nah,' he said. 'Just a bit of business.'

'So -' I paused. I hoped I'd not just overheard a torture murder. 'Ed's not going to pay his rent until the work's done. Do you know when it might be finished?'

'Don't worry pal. I'm on my way over there now. Just need to clear the mattress then I'll be off.'

Clear the mattress? What did he mean? I daren't ask lest he break my kneecaps. 'Okay,' I said. 'Could you let me know when it's finished?'

'Course pal.' Another ear-splitting scream. Another *crack*. 'I'll give you a bell when I'm done.'

'Okay thanks.' I said, quickly hanging up. Interestingly,

I dreamt about that scream for the next forty years.

Instead of drinking myself blind today I thought I'd visit Sheena in the cafe and give her the good news. She'd surely be thrilled to know she could soon throw her job back in the owner's face and buy her own cow meat. But who'd then feed the wife? I imagined he'd hire a new minion or - should that prove too expensive - simply leave her to starve.

I ordered a taxi and loafed about the building lobby till it arrived. The doorman stood sternly to attention, his trousers pressed and static. There was a dark patch on his jacket where I'd hit him with an orange the previous day.

'Hello doorman.' I said.

'Morning sir.' He didn't look me in the eye, instead staring past me with a tired and doleful hatred.

'I'm waiting for a taxi,' I said. 'Should be here soon.'

'Very good sir.' He stood very still, chin raised and hands behind his back like a police lineup suspect.

I paced the lobby, admiring of the extravagantly-spined plants that lined the walls. Should we fill our flat with such shrubs? Would the doorman water them for us? I wondered what he did in the evenings and felt strangely saddened. Probably a bone collector, I thought.

My taxi drew up outside. 'Bye doorman.' I said, striding to the glass entrance.

'Goodbye sir.' he said, his hatred unswerving and steadfast.

The taxi driver puttered into town, asking if I minded him stopping to use the lavatory in a roadside ditch. *That's fine*, I said, not expecting him to unfunnel a horsemound of excrement into the ferns. He wiped himself with a carrier bag and returned to the car, blubbered and pale with sweat. 'Sorry about that,' he said. 'Bad cow meat at lunch.'

I sympathised, repulsed by the smell of manure he'd brought back with him.

'You can't trust a lot of places these days,' he said, presumably warming up to a racial slur. 'If you know what

I mean.'

I assured him I had no idea what he meant, and would he mind being quiet because I had a terrible headache.

'Say no more, fella, say no more,' he said. 'Some people got no respect. Up all night doing this and that. Not like the old days.'

Shut up, racist, I thought, trying not to catch his eye. (Might he indoctrinate me into a hate group?) I'd noticed a trend among white service workers to envision The Past as a bountiful period of economic and cultural prosperity, untarnished by the tolerance we enjoy today.

'People used to have some respect.' he said, exasperatedly shaking his head. He was being deliberately opaque, presumably to avoid being reported for hate speech at work (I'd report him anyway). 'But that's all gone out the bloody window.'

He mithered about his health visitor not speaking perfect English ('it's a bloody disgrace'), despite being in no position to criticise the parlance of others. I hummed disinterestedly. *I'll not be ensnared in your web of prejudice,* I thought, wondering if he gave discounts to white supremacists.

We arrived at Muggins Cafe and I resentfully handed him cash, all of which I assumed he'd spend on football scarves and white power CDs. (He refused debit card payments, fearful of government surveillance.)

'Be careful in there, fella,' he said, implying I was staging some kind of raid.

Thanks, I grimaced. *Now go and kill yourself.*

Inside was busier than my last visit, probably due to the lunchtime rush. Scanning the room I noted Sheena was right, the customers *were* disgusting. Mainly builders with plaster grey faces, speckled with paint and dirt, all drinking tea and slurping rubbery egg whites. Racist newspapers littered the tables and hard hats took up all available floor space. Several dogs tramped about, gobbling scraps and waiting hungrily for their owners to die.

Sheena was in the kitchen, sweating like a newspaper editor and red as a strawberry frog. She was dicing meat with a kitchen shovel while simultaneously gobbing on each meal the owner passed her, like a ketchup dispenser blasting the lunches with concentrated squirts of phlegm.

'Sheena,' I said, jostling through the troglodyte mass. 'Can I talk to you? It's good news.'

She nodded to the staff entrance, gesturing that she'd be there in a minute. There was a disgruntled shuffle as she abandoned her post; a resigned grousing as those in the queue realised their butties would be microscopically delayed. *Simmer down, scum,* I thought.

'What's going on?' said Sheena, gulping two whisky miniatures she produced from her apron. 'Has that prick paid us yet or what?'

'Not yet,' I said. 'But Handyman's promised he'll finish it today. We should be fine by tomorrow.'

She lit a Thrushman's. 'Thank Christ for that,' she said. '*Finally* I can get out of this shithole.'

There was loud dissent from the counter: the owner was struggling to cook, spit on, and serve the requisite butties in a timely fashion. 'I'd better go,' she said, stubbing her cig out on a binbag of fish. She dashed off before hesitating. 'While you're here -' she said, 'would you mind feeding the wife? She's in the cellar. I'd do it myself but we're swamped right now.' Before I could protest she'd handed me a padlock key and pointed to an unmarked door. 'Down the steps, you can't miss her,' she said. 'Scraps from the compost bin, leave 'em in the bowl, refill the water bucket, easy. Takes two minutes. There's a mop down there as well. For the piss.'

I stood in the filthy service corridor with a woman's freedom in the palm of my hand. Should I let her go? I'd play it by ear, I thought. Grabbing a fistful of compost I clanked open the padlock and thrust the door open, wincing at its harrowing screech. Closing it behind me I was queased by the darkness, a tense reminder of

Grandma's first abduction. Inside was warm and smelt like woodchip and manure, surprising as I'd more expected the tangy stench of urine. Clearly Sheena had done a good job of mopping up.

Descending the steps I fumbled for a handrail and felt one lagging from the wall. It was sticky, probably from blood or corn oil, and my palm peeled away as if from a pub carpet.

'Hello wife?' I called. 'Mrs -' I paused, what was her name? 'Mrs Muggins? I'm here to feed you compost scraps.' My words echoed in the gloom.

The cellar was dank and soured with vegetable matter. The walls ran wet with condensation and there were styrofoam crates piled carelessly on top of each other. I noticed some were pocked with holes - probably the prisoner hunting for snacks. I scanned the sawdusted floor and located the feeding bowl. 'Lunchtime Mrs Muggins!' I called, depositing the scraps. Silence. Presumably she'd become more reclusive since her incarceration, I thought, refilling her water bucket and edging back up the staircase. I ignored the urine mop (Sheena could deal with that) and reached the door. With my hand on the knob I stiffened (not due to arousal), having heard a noise. A shuffling from the cellar, deep amongst the crates. Mrs Muggins?

Open up! I thought, yanking at the door. It was jammed somehow. The shuffling became clearer, now also taking in licks and smacking sounds. She must be eating, I thought, somewhat famished myself. I had a packet of hare legs in the fridge so thought maybe I'd have those for lunch (the bones would be thrown at the doorman) while Sheena had left a half bottle of traffickers' rum in the sink, an afternoon treat I'd glug like a parched baby.

The door finally scraped open and I wriggled outside. Closing it behind me I heard a tiny voice from inside. 'Bye,' it said, almost inaudibly. 'Come back soon.'

No thanks, I thought, replacing the padlock and dashing back to the kitchen. Sheena was hard at work: frying,

41

spitting, frying, spitting, frying, spitting. I handed her the key and mechanically she spat on my hand.

'All done,' I said, wiping the phlegm on a nearby customer's jacket. 'Fed and watered.'

'Oh thanks,' she said, shaken from her drill. 'Saves me doing it. Did she give you any trouble?'

'No,' I said. 'Actually she asked me to come back soon.'

'Ha!' said Sheena. 'Sounds about right. Yesterday she asked me for a clean pair of pants. What am I, the fucking chambermaid?'

No, I said, staring hungrily at the cow meat, tender and grey under the heat lamps.

'See you at home then.' she said.

Yes, I said. *See you then.*

~

I ate the hare legs straight out of the packet, ignoring the boiling guidelines and salmonella warnings. They were sinewy and tasted like gunpowder. Once finished, I went to the balcony and threw the bones at the doorman as planned, aiming to knock his hat off but instead hitting a neighbour's car.

'Next time sir.' he called, waving a gloved hand.

I drank the trafficker's rum and fell into an exhausted slump in front of the telly. I watched a programme about kindly bailiffs and wondered which of Ed's possessions I could legitimately seize. His computer would surely sell for a few hundred, all money I could spend on mohair scarves. I'd also noticed a bicycle in the hallway, probably worth thousands. How did he afford such luxuries? Sheena said he worked with digital computers and I considered getting an application form before falling into a drunken stupor.

CHAPTER 9

Today was the big day. I was on the phone to Handyman confirming the work was all done (binbag stapled, refrigerator shoved in) and would be awaiting Ed when he returned from work.

'I done it as cheaply as I could,' he said. 'Shittest of everything.'

'Perfect.' I said. Despite his truculent manner, Handyman was a dependable cohort in such scenarios, even, I believed, taking a perverse pleasure in inconveniencing people he deemed lofty or intellectual.

He'd performed appallingly at school, expelled after torturing classmates and cutting teachers' brake cables (eight dead, twelve hospitalised) and sent to borstal. While incarcerated he'd learned various drilling techniques and, upon release, graduated to house repairs and casual burglary. I knew little else about him besides his penchant for torture (it 'nourished him like fire') and the fact he may once have been a people trafficker, a practice he defended as being 'cheaper than train travel.'

I was eager to end the call and avoid any discussion of his fee.

'Money.' he said, anticipating my evasionary tactics. 'I only take cash. I'll be round tomorrow.'

I tensed like a fried mollusc. 'Okay.' I said, clueless as

to how we'd pay him. *You'd better cough up immediately, Ed,* I thought, knowing Handyman wouldn't hesitate for a second before jamming a chisel in my guts. An invaluable asset when in your employ, his viciousness was admirably democratic, turning like a gun turret on anyone who dared cross him. (He'd once buried a man alive for stealing his dustbin.)

He hung up and I sat, hungover and pensive, waiting for payment confirmation. It was early afternoon and Sheena was at work, presumably gobbing on sausages, while Ed would be working digitally somewhere (the future?). With little else to do I spent an hour tenderising my ballsack and nibbling pork skirt.

'What's the news?' said Sheena, waking me up three hours later. 'Has he paid? Little tosser.'

She was right, he *was* a little tosser. I especially hated his fluffy beard and predilection for cycling caps. 'I'll check the account.' I said, flipping open the computer.

Sheena was shaking as she poured her afternoon livener, a half-pint measure of prison wine and bread pulp that she wolfed down immediately, claiming she'd been 'stressed' at work and needed to black out as soon as possible. 'Had to change the wife's knickers,' she said between frantic gulps. 'Smelt like a hamster cage.'

I was silent as she talked. 'She kept saying she'd be leaving soon. That people were coming to take her away. Don't know if she's gone mad or what.'

I beckoned to her with a shuddering hand.

'What's the matter?' she said, skittering over with her drink already half done.

Ratcheting up the tension I pointed at the screen.

Her mouth opened softly. 'At *last*.' she whispered, staring at our available balance. 'Little bastard's paid up.'

Not only had Ed paid this month's rent early, he'd also coughed up for last month as well. She bolted her drink and sucked my cheek with a kiss. 'Yes!' she cried. 'We won!'

We subsequently got roaring drunk, hurling bottles from the balcony and chaining cigs like it was wartime. 'So Handyman must've done a decent job,' she said, launching a tumbler at the doorman. 'That didn't take long.'

I was sure there was more to it than that. Ed didn't seem the type to simply comply without a squabble, nor did I believe Handyman had done even a semblance of a decent job. Why had he suddenly given us what we wanted?

'Who cares,' she said. 'We got our money. Now I can leave that shit job. Time to celebrate.'

That night I ended up drunker than I'd been in weeks. I woke up on Sheena's bedroom floor, naked and crusted with albumen. What on earth had happened? I hauled myself to the kitchen with a head like granite and a mouth like a bird's nest. Had I eaten a rat? I thrust open the cold tap and drank enough to waterboard a political whistleblower. Refreshed but in abject agony, I curled up on the sofa and tried to cry but hadn't any residual moisture.

I tried to piece the evening together. I'd felt intense elation at the news of Ed's payment, and consequently resolved to get as wrecked as possible. It was an almost overwhelming rush of relief knowing Sheena could leave her job, that we could pay Handyman, and that our income was secured for the foreseeable future. We'd ordered a case of gin from Sloshford's - an online delivery service that confiscated its drivers' passports and paid them in bottletops - and guzzled enough to bring down a brachiosaur.

My brain had shut down early but my body had somehow remained functional, evidently a contributing factor in the field of debris outside. Leaning over the railing, it seemed we'd thrown glasses, lamps, tins, cutlery and dinner plates out of the window, the remnants of which the doorman was dutifully sweeping up, his face grey with the sleepless exhaustion of a new parent. 'Good morning sir.' he said, noticing me leaning over the balcony. He didn't smile.

'Hello doorman.' I said. 'Are you having a nice day?' *Why had I said that? Was I still drunk?*

He put down his binbag and looked up at me, revealing a red gash down the side of his head. Had we hit him with a bottle? 'Yes sir.' he said, stemming the blood with a handkerchief.

'Oh great,' I said, definitely still drunk. 'Keep up the good work.'

I closed the curtains and went straight back to bed.

~

My precious snooze was interrupted by an incessant thumping at the door. Had the reaper come for me at last? Surely hell couldn't be any worse than my current situation, I thought, my brain scraping like punctured metal. My sheets were saturated and I smelt like a corpse flower, all rot and atrophy. *Lead me to the grave, reaper*, I thought, struggling to the front door.

I was met by the dishevelled face of Handyman. He was smoking a petrol cig and breathed a huge gust in my face. 'Money.' he said.

My neck tensed as a geyser of sick came piping up my throat. I swallowed deeply, managing not to spew on his overalls.

He shoved me aside and barged into the flat, knocking over a plant pot as I choked down a second rush of vomit. He took a seat at the kitchen table. 'Get me my money.' he said. 'Now.' He was so terrifying that I wanted to curl up like a foetus and roll out of the window.

'Can I do a bank transfer?' I said, fully aware he might punch me in the face.

He stubbed his cig out on the carpet and lit another immediately. 'Money.' he said again, this time with yellow slime snaking from his mouth. I was genuinely frightened.

Should I call Sheena? She was still unconscious, poor thing. Maybe I'd fry her some cow meat later, I thought, as kindly as a caregiver.

'I've not got it in cash I'm afraid,' I said. 'If you give me your bank details I could do a direct debit -'

'Cash.' he said. 'I ain't gonna ask you again.'

'Okay but I'll need to go to a cash machine,' I said. 'The nearest one's in Plugwood Lock. I'd need to phone for a taxi.' I hoped my sluggish procrastination would deter him enough to leave me alone, for I was tired and deserved an afternoon in bed.

'I'll drive.' he said. 'Van's outside. Get some pants on.'

Was this a dream? Was I really being shepherded to a cash machine in a disgusting tradesman's van? 'Okay then,' I said. 'Give me an hour, to freshen up and whatnot.'

'You've got five minutes.' he said. 'Otherwise I'm dragging you there myself.'

I left him spitting fag ends into the sink and went off to dress myself. Five minutes wasn't *nearly* enough - I needed time to apply corn butter and source my favourite cashmere.

'Two minutes.' he called, before I knew what was happening. 'Then we're going.'

Christ, Handyman, I thought. Evidently five minutes was enough for him to haul on a grouting smock but I had a routine. 'Coming.' I said, uncrumpling my trousers and pulling on a sturdy cable knit. It wasn't stab-proof but I had no Kevlar to hand (why had I given up fencing?) and thought the wool fibres would cushion any wounds he might inflict.

I reappeared in the living room just as he was about to smash a window. 'Stop!' I said. 'I'm ready!'

He lowered his clawhammer and frogmarched me out of the apartment. We bounded down the stairs and emerged in the lobby. The doorman was standing by the lift, brushing his moustache with a flat comb and humming a communist song. 'Good afternoon, sir.' he said.

'Hello doorman,' I said. 'Just going for a drive.'

'Very good sir.' he said with a scowl. He had a bruise on his forehead where Sheena had hit him with a tin of butterbeans last night.

'Cheers pal,' said Handyman, thrusting a banknote at him. 'See y'again.'

'Very kind of you sir,' said the doorman, tipping him his hat. 'Let me get that for you.' He swung open the door and waved Handyman through, leaving it to thump closed in my face. They both laughed as blood plunged from my nose, soddening my knitwear and leaving me spinning. 'I'm so sorry sir,' said the doorman, handing me a soiled napkin. 'Rotten luck.'

Absolute bastard, I thought, resolving to get him sacked as soon as possible.

We approached Handyman's shitheap of a van and I wondered if I'd ever see daylight again. *Don't overreact*, I told myself. *All he wants is money.* To my surprise he nodded to the passenger door (I assumed he'd bundle me into the back like a poached cockerel) and grunted something about seatbelts. I climbed inside and recoiled at the smell: cigs, sweat, dust sheets, lager, farts. The ashtray jutted out like an underbite, bulging with fag ends and volcanic quantities of ash. My seatbelt looked like it'd been shredded by a trapped beast, hanging loosely around my belly like a maypole garland.

'Bastard nearly escaped.' said Handyman cryptically, nodding at the gnawed belt. He growled under his breath as he gunned the ignition.

Predictably he drove like a maniac, veering to hit foxes and cyclists and cursing as they escaped unhurt. 'Did that little prick pay you?' he said, lighting two cigs.

'Yes,' I said. 'He paid us yesterday actually.'

'Haha,' he wheezed. 'Course he did.'

What did you do, Handyman? I thought, envisaging bloody scenes of torture. Was Ed even still alive?

'I gave 'im a little nudge.' he said, cackling to himself.

I probed no further, lest I was asked to recount the conversation in court.

We drove through Crumbford, a terrifying wasteland whose high street now housed only estate agents and military salvage emporiums. On a street corner a group of children threw cats at cars, shrieking when they hit a windscreen and the driver screeched uncontrollably off course.

We continued on, past abandoned petrol stations, industrial wasteground and flat-roofed hate pubs draped in national flags.

'Broke a guy's neck in there once.' he said, nodding to one such pub, its windows frosted like a pornographer's. 'That was a good laugh.'

We pulled up outside a bank in Plugwood and he kept the van running. 'Don't be long.' he said.

I stood in line for the cash machine, thrilled that Handyman would soon be off my back.

I withdrew his bloodmoney and thrust it through the driver's window. 'No need to count it.' I said, but he counted it anyway.

'Good. Phone if you need anything else doing.' he said, gulping from a flask.

Suddenly I became aware of something shifting in the back of the van. It was a hessian sack positioned behind the driver's seat, inconspicuous among the ladders and paint buckets. It stirred very slowly, making a light groaning sound. Handyman heard it and snapped back to the steering wheel. 'Shit,' he said. 'He's woken up. Gotta go.' He revved the engine and roared away, leaving me choking on claggy clouds of petrol.

Thank heavens *that* was dealt with, I thought, daydreaming of salmon en croute.

CHAPTER 10

We quickly returned to a state of languid normalcy. Neither of us woke before midday, nor, for several weeks, did we even change out of our pyjamas. Why on earth should we?

Sheena was particularly ebullient, for she'd endured the grind of gainful employment and was now basking in the afterglow of resignation. Instead of handing in her notice, she'd simply not bothered turning up to work, a strategy that'd elicited fury from the cafe owner, mostly because he was now required to mop up his wife's faeces.

Happily, I'd been drinking more and my aim had vastly improved. I was now able to hit the doorman with a whole range of projectiles: onions, fish heads, marrowbones - often knocking his hat off with marksmanlike accuracy. 'Good shot, sir.' he'd say, wiping blood plasma from his uniform.

Ed had also quietened down considerably, silenced by Handyman's grave and mysterious counsel. He kept out of our way, moaning only when he discovered human liver remnants in a freezer compartment. 'Tell him to fry them for his mum's birthday.' said Sheena, utterly unconcerned for his wellbeing. She'd suggested, early in the tenancy, that we coat the ceilings with asbestos in an effort to beleaguer his respiratory system later in life. 'The symptoms take years to appear,' she said. 'He'd never know it was us.' Naturally I was in full agreement, but unfortunately Handyman had sold his last batch to a contractor responsible for government social housing. Apparently it formed part of a council initiative designed to weaken, and eventually kill, residents before they hoovered up too many local resources. 'I don't know why they don't just use firing squads.' said Sheena.

Life was good, although it wouldn't be so for long. We were idling one afternoon; me ordering piano whisks, Sheena picking scabs, when the phone rang. 'Tell them to piss off.' she said, draped on a balcony chair with a cocktail.

Phone calls were always bad. Always either Stu, Handyman or the cafe owner mithering about money or obligations or responsibility, none of which now concerned us given our renewed solvency. Often I'd pick up the phone and make gargling noises until the caller disconnected through frustration or disgust. I picked up the receiver. 'Gharbleughalala,' I gurgled.

'Hello?' came the voice. It was so officious I found myself apologising,

'Who are you apologising to?' shouted Sheena. 'Tell them to get off my pissing phone!'

I covered my ear and held the phone close. 'Sorry about that.' I said. 'How can I help?'

He introduced himself as a police officer and continued, warm but efficient: 'Do you know an Edward Partleton-Greene?'

Yes, I said, despite wishing I didn't. 'He's my tenant.' Had Ed reported us to Plod? Whatever for?

'I'm afraid I've got some bad news,' he said. 'He's been involved in an accident.'

I couldn't help but smile and snigger. 'That's awful,' I said. 'What happened?'

'Gas explosion. Very nasty. He's in intensive care. It's not looking good I'm afraid. Were you aware of a gas leak at the property?'

Uh-oh, I thought. Which part of this should I lie about?

'Hello?' said the officer. 'Are you still there?'

'Yes.' I said. My back was sweating. I needed a Thrushman's. Could I get Sheena's attention?

'Were you aware of a gas leak at the property?' he repeated.

I faltered, stuttered, dithered. If I said *yes* I'd be in some way responsible for Ed's hospitalisation, potentially even his death. If I said *no* I'd be found out and horsewhipped for lying to Plod. What a rotten position to be in, I thought, resentful of Plod's tedious do-gooding. Potentially the most worrying factor was my implicating Handyman. I could feasibly lay the blame at his feet ('he told me it was safe,' etc.) but couldn't guarantee he'd not rip my bones out in return. In order to stall things, I pleaded ignorance, hoping it'd cause him more paperwork.

'No,' I said. 'I had no idea. There was a *gas leak?* That's terrible.'

'I'm afraid so,' he said. 'Pretty bad. Whole place went off.'

My first thought was for the flat. Would this affect the resale value? 'Was there much damage?' I said, trying not to sound too insensitive.

'We can go through all that later,' he said, as if anything mattered more than my precious investment. 'First we need to assess the property, rule out anything suspicious.'

This was worrying. If Plod found out about Handyman's botch job I'd be thrown in prison and forced to stitch trainers for sportswear corporations.

'So we'll probably be contacting you again,' he said. 'Make sure you keep your phone on.'

I resolved immediately to throw the phone off the balcony. 'Of course.' I said.

I returned to Sheena, antsy and spooked.

'What's the matter?' she said. 'You look weird.'

'That was Plod on the phone,' I said. 'There's been an

explosion. At the flat. Ed's in hospital.'

'Oh my *god*,' she said, spilling her drink as she shot up from the chair. 'Is the flat okay? Will this affect the resale value?'

I told her what Plod had told me. She was justifiably thrilled at Ed's incapacitation ('no more moaning about fridges') but, like me, aggrieved at the damage that'd been caused.

'It's that handyman,' she spat. 'He screwed us. Why didn't he fix that gas leak?'

'I know,' I said. 'It's awful. But what can we do?'

My question was answered promptly by Plod, two of whom dropped by a couple of days later with devastating news. Despite the coma, Ed was now stable, clinging to life like a troublesome head louse. The flat, however, had been classified as uninhabitable by a gaggle of meddlesome bureaucrats. Obviously I assumed there'd been some kind of administrative error, as it was clearly perfectly liveable.

'We've had the safety assessment back,' said Plod. 'And I'm afraid that's not the case. The surveyor advised the place be condemned.'

'That's rubbish.' said Sheena. 'It's a bloody palace!'

Plod leaned forward in his seat, his face focused and taut. He was lean like an astronaut and had a jawbone like a cinderblock. 'Now I don't know if you're aware, but negligence like this is a criminal offence. You've caused life-threatening injuries to your tenant, and I'm afraid I'm going to have to place you both under arrest.'

And that was it. Just like that, we were criminals. Actual, certifiable criminals. Despite the indiscretions of my past (blackmail, drug dealing, accessory to murder), I'd never considered myself a *real* criminal, simply because I'd never done anything empirically wrong. Plod may have thought differently, but I knew I'd always acted with honour and integrity, brave and principled and brilliant. Now, however, my reputation was tarnished and I'd likely end up cuffed to a radiator and beaten senseless with sex truncheons.

They read us our rights (*yawn*) and led us to the car. 'Get off me!' shrieked Sheena. 'And get me a bottle of cava!'

'One for me too.' I said. Might they have Gran Cuvee? We'd been so coddled by Stu it felt insulting not being lavished with premium fizz at every juncture. Evidently Plod wanted us to suffer, offering little in the way of refreshments.

'Enough of that, you two,' they said. 'You'll not be getting any of that for a while.'

'Plod, listen to me,' said Sheena. 'I'm parched. You didn't even let me finish my cocktail. We have to stop at an off licence on the way to prison, or wherever the hell we're going.'

They shook their heads exasperatedly, implying she was somehow being unreasonable. *I hate you Plod*, I thought, recalling the unpleasantness of years earlier. (I'd been made a drug mule for this very constabulary, and was remunerated so poorly I'd barely been able to afford a decent espresso machine.)

We crunched up to the police station and were marched inside like gulag initiates. Heartbreakingly, Plod offered us neither nibbles nor sparkling wine. We weren't even offered *lager*. Instead we were presented to a custody sergeant who took our details and authorised our detention.

'You do know we've done nothing wrong?' said Sheena, lying like a parliamentarian. 'That flat was fit for a king. We had *noblemen* queuing up to rent that place.'

The sergeant ignored her, instead completing wearisome forms and instructing we remove our belts and shoelaces.

'Why?' she raged. 'So you can beat us with them? No thanks.'

He advised it was to reduce the risk of suicide, clearly unfamiliar with Sheena's former deathwish.

'If I wanted to kill myself there'd be nothing you could do to stop me.' she said, before adding, somewhat ominously, 'I've only got one lung.'

Perhaps due to my previous experiences with Plod, I remained silent throughout this exchange, instead staring about the room like a thicko. Next we were searched and our treasured possessions (cigs, vodka miniatures) confiscated for Plod's use later that night. I envisioned them loafing around a card table like snails, drunk on our booze and chuffing our cigs, concocting ways to exasperate our suffering by whipping us and capping our sushi ration. Could I survive on sashimi alone?

We weren't entitled to a phone call (a media-made myth, apparently) but they could contact someone to notify them of our arrest and tell them where we were. Additionally, we were offered free legal advice, a gesture of pity we immediately declined.

'Phone Stu,' said Sheena. 'He knows a lawyer. The estate agents use him all the time. Slippery little rat apparently.'

Thus we found ourselves languishing in separate cells, glumly awaiting the company lawyer. According to Stu he was the property industry's preeminent legal snake, with over two hundred ruinations to his name. He also boasted a portfolio of clients that'd unnerve Satan himself: lettings agents, payday lenders, slum landlords: beleaguered service providers all given the freedom to operate by kindly ministers who, like us, were simply trying to safeguard their investments.

The police cell was white and peeling, with a bunk and a small lavatory into which I assumed Plod submerged prisoners' heads during nightly torture raids. I stared about me and wondered how many footballers had stewed in here after hitting bystanders with sports cars or savaging bouncers with bike chains. If only I held some sway with the beer-guzzling general public, I thought, I too might get off with a slap on the wrists. I needed to rid my head of such pipe dreams and think clearly. What would I tell Plod? What would Sheena tell Plod?

The gas safety certificate had obviously expired, they'd have no trouble corroborating that. Then they'd ask why we'd not renewed it, to which we'd have no answer. Stu had told us, repeatedly, to renew the certificate, and we'd always said *yeah yeah whatever where's the cava*, but he'd been absolutely right. Why hadn't we listened?

We *could* claim ignorance, but infuriatingly this was no excuse. How the hell was I supposed to know every detail of the rulebook? Was I a solicitor?

It seemed we were in a corner, and this time I couldn't see a way out.

CHAPTER 11

The lawyer's name was Hilary Bell. He was brittle and thin, like his bones were held together with coathangers, and his suit looked like it cost more than Mum's rage therapy.

He sat down in the cell and shook my hand. 'I'm Hilary Bell,' he said. 'Let's get you out of here, shall we?'

We sat in an interview room opposite Plod, and Hilary Bell advised I answer *no comment* to absolutely everything. Plod were hugely frustrated by this but there was little they could do without further investigation. Hilary Bell negotiated our bail and we were out within an hour.

'Honestly, I thought we were bollocked.' said Sheena, skipping towards the taxi. 'What did you tell them?'

Hilary Bell laughed, a reedy, malevolent snicker. 'Let's just say I've got some good contacts.' he said, swinging his car door open. 'Maybe you'd like to meet them? I think they'd be your kind of people.'

'What do you mean?' she said. 'Who's our kind of people?'

He slipped into the driver's seat (camel leather, seat warmer) and leaned, skeletal, out of the window. 'You'll find out. Stay local, okay?' He waved goodbye and purred off, advising us his bill would be in the post.

'The least Stu could've done is pay our legal bill,' said Sheena. 'He's the reason we're in this mess.'

'Is he?' I said, struggling with her logic.

'Of course, he sent us that handyman, didn't he? He's the reason this all happened.'

I was tired and thus assumed she was right. Maybe it *was* all Stu's fault. How could we implicate him?

'We need to make sure he pays for this,' she said, clawing at her cashmere. 'You can't trust an estate agent.'

On this point she was right. When they'd first arrived on earth, estate agents were little more than subservient underlings, docile chimps facilitating the sale of houses. Once they'd learned humanity's weaknesses, however, they'd resolved to bleed us like livestock. They'd concluded that humans required shelter, heating and a water source to survive, usually contained within the walls of a residential building. Given the housing market was laughably unregulated, they'd conspired to swindle the population out of its earnings, weakening and demoralising the population. I could only assume their end goal was some kind of global mass suicide, a self-extermination of millions of impoverished rent slaves who've realised the futility of working themselves into a pauper's grave.

We laid low for the next few days, terrified of a knocking door or ringing phone. Hilary Bell's cryptic comment about 'our kind of people' had left us anxious. What could he possibly mean? Landlords? Martyrs?

A week later there was, as feared, a knock at the door. Not a pounding, but a firm and measured rap. Sheena was slumped in a chair and jumped like a startled coot. 'Who's that?' she said. 'Plod?'

I had no idea. We'd heard nothing since being arrested, a humiliating error I attributed to government police cuts.

I straggled to the door and glared through the peephole. There stood a man, white-haired, with a grandfatherly moustache and a wool rich tie. Had uncle Sid returned from hell?

'Who is it?' whispered Sheena. 'The lawyer?'

I shook my head.

'Stu?'

I flapped my arms. *I don't know!* I mouthed.

The knocking again. 'Is anyone there?' came a voice. It was warm and arch like a rubber baron's.

What do I do? I gesticulated, panicking.

Sheena sat glued to her seat, her jaw clenched. She mouthed again, more aggressively this time. *Tell him to piss off!*

'Listen, I know you've had a few problems recently,' said the voice. 'That business with your tenant sounded just ghastly.' How did he know about Ed? 'But I'm not here to trouble you. I want to help you.'

Sheena and I looked at each other. He clearly knew we were at home. Realising we had little choice, we exchanged a consenting nod and I unlocked the door. Standing before me I took in the full length of the man. His hands were cupped confidently behind his back and his chest puffed out like a Yorkshire pudding. He beamed at me and extended a fat hand. 'Horton Wretchley.' he said, his voice like tobacco and fudge. 'Pleased to meet you.' Mildly unnerved, I shook his hand and invited him in. He strode to Sheena and bowed before her. 'A pleasure.' he said, pecking her hand.

What's going on? she mouthed behind his back. Again, I shrugged. I had no idea.

'Mind if I rest my legs, dear? The old spine's not what it used to be. I feel like a bloody beached whale.'

'Oh, of course,' she said, gesturing to a chair. 'Would you like a drink?'

'You're too kind.' he said. 'I'd go *doolally* for a scotch. Traffic was terrible, you see.'

I poured him a huge measure and one for myself (Sheena was already half drunk).

'That's the ticket,' he said, polishing it off. 'My tongue was as dry as an Iraqi prison.' Was he being racist? I wasn't sure.

'You said you wanted to help us,' said Sheena,

interrupting my boring thoughts. 'Help us with what?'

Wretchley snapped open a cigarette case. 'You don't mind, do you?' he said. 'I'm absolutely clucking for a gasper.' We all lit cigs (his smelled of rosewater and cedarwood, ours like charred hair) and clinked glasses. He was inordinately confident, effortlessly eliciting our admiration and respect. Was it the moustache?

'Yes yes, to business,' he said, languorously exhaling a cerulean plume. 'Mustn't dither, must we? Lots to do.'

'What business are you talking about?' said Sheena. 'Who are you?'

'I'm a member of a little club,' he said. 'And I thought it might be something you'd enjoy. It's all very low-key, of course, we meet once a month, have a good bleth, that kind of thing.'

'What do you bleth about?' I said, enraptured by his caginess.

He eyed me conspiratorially. 'Oh everything. Life, work, property. Things that'd interest you.'

We looked at each other. Did he want to sell us into the sex trade? 'Is it a sex thing?' said Sheena.

'Good heavens, no,' he laughed, a thick, wheezing guffaw that sounded like a steam train. 'It's more like a forum, I suppose, somewhere to meet like-minded people. People like you.'

That expression again: *people like you*. What did it mean?

'What do you mean by that?' said Sheena, now mildly angry. Once the alcohol took hold her patience shrivelled like a cold scrotum. 'Why do people keep saying that?'

'My dear, I wish I could elaborate but I simply can't. Not now.' He handed her a card embossed with paisley ridging. 'Everything's on there, okay? I do hope you can make it.'

Something in his tone, with its unhurried, rosy authority, stopped us from needling further. He rose briskly, his face plummy and ruddied, and shook our hands. 'Must dash now, heaps to get through,' he said. 'It's been a bloody pleasure though. I look forward to our meeting again.'

Once he'd gone we dashed to the balcony, hoping to catch a further glimpse of our visitor. There was a black saloon parked in front of the building, the driver of which held the door open as Wretchley disappeared inside.

'So -' said Sheena. 'What the hell was that about?'

'I don't know,' I said, absentmindedly hurling a beer can at the doorman. 'He seemed to like us though.'

'Yes, he did,' she said, notably suspicious. 'I wonder why.'

We drank ourselves to sleep watching a programme about working-class cake munchers who were confronted by their gluttony and made to cry. 'Why don't they just kill themselves?' said Sheena, a lit cig up her nose. 'That's what I'd do.'

'Me too.' I said.

~

Several weeks after our incarceration we received a court summons. Our case had gone to trial and, incredibly, we were being tried for criminal negligence. Compounding this insult were whispers of involuntary manslaughter should Ed not wake from his coma.

Panicked, we'd come to Hilary Bell's office to assess our options and formulate some kind of defence. It was a tasteful suite in a sharded glass building overlooking Plugwood Broadway, an affluent city stretch on which business people sloshed coffee over the homeless. Atop his cabinets were trophies, stuffed wolves and volumes of tedious law books, all fodder for the nearest bonfire. On the wall was a framed photo of an electric chair, apparently in memory of the first man he'd sent to his death.

'Let me assure you, you've nothing to worry about,' he said, sipping fennel water. 'You're not killers. Just homeowners with a nose for a saving.'

'That's absolutely right,' said Sheena. 'But how can you be so confident? How do you know we'll not be thrown in jail with a load of variety comedians?'

'Trust me,' he said. 'You'll be fine.'

Despite sounding as deluded as a royalist, somehow I trusted him to get us off the hook. Perhaps it was his slender frog fingers or extortionate hourly rate, but something about him put me very much at ease. 'Well, if you think so,' I said. 'There doesn't seem to be much to worry about.'

'That's the spirit,' he said, crossing his bamboo-thin legs. 'Nothing to worry about. Just turn up to court on the day, try not to get drunk beforehand, and we'll hash this all out. I'm sure it's just a big misunderstanding.'

Thus we left with yet *another* problem before us: the court hearing was on a Friday, and on Fridays we started drinking in the morning and didn't stop till we were chundering into slop buckets.

'Maybe we could get twice as drunk the night before.' said Sheena, her resourcefulness shining like a supermoon. 'That way we'd still be drunk the next morning. Go to the hearing, start drinking straight afterwards. Easy.'

It was a great plan. It meant we'd not suffer a minute of sobriety the whole day, yet couldn't technically be accused of drinking the morning before our trial.

'I don't know why you can't drink in court anyway.' she said, sipping from a tin of wood lacquer.

'I know, it's bonkers.' I said, swept up in her madness. Did she really believe the things she said?

'My taxes *paid* for that courtroom.' she said, sounding distinctly like a taxi-driving racist. What next? Would she start lambasting nurses for whom English was a second language?

'Mmm,' I murmured, eager to steer the conversation elsewhere. 'Shall we head home?'

'Bollocks to that,' she said. 'Let's go and get shitfaced.'

This unseated me, for traditionally we'd get shitfaced at

home. Why should we go elsewhere?

'There's a pub down there,' she said, pointing vaguely down the street. 'The Pig & Bucket. The bar manager's got Lyme disease.'

'Is it nice?' I said, assuming not.

'It is when you've got money in your pocket.' she said, flattering my ego and thus garnering my compliance.

'Okay,' I said. 'Let's go.'

We slouched up to the bar, ordered six whiskies and necked them in quick succession.

'We need to do this more often,' said Sheena, her words strangled and sloppy. 'Why do we always stay at home to drink?'

I'd never fully considered this before. Perhaps, subconsciously or otherwise, we felt we'd fought so hard for the apartment it'd be wasteful to spend any time away from it. It could've also been attributable to our ingrained frugality, born from years spent destitute, that forbade us from paying for a pint of lager what could feasibly afford us a half bottle of supermarket vodka.

'I really don't know,' I said. 'Maybe we hate people?'

She nodded. 'I know I do.'

We took a table and tried to adjust to the atmosphere of a public space. It was comfortable enough, though not as comfortable as home, and the drinks were weaker than if we'd poured them ourselves.

'How do people *do* this?' said Sheena. 'It's so expensive.'

'I don't know,' I said. 'Maybe they've got some kind of rationing system, like during the war.'

'You mean they're given a ration book for lager?'

'Yes, I imagine so,' I said. 'Otherwise how would they afford it?'

'You're right,' she said. 'Thank God we're minted.'

'Thank God.'

We spent the equivalent of a month's rent on drinks, racking them up like we were in mainland Europe. We were asked to leave after Sheena threw her glass at a bar worker's head, assuming the same rules applied as with the doorman. 'This is ridiculous!' she screamed as the manager heaved her out to the street. 'I've done nothing wrong!'

'You're lucky I don't call the police.' he said, helpfully saving us from an assault charge. 'Good thing you spent so much money in here tonight.'

'Seriously, what did I *do?*' Sheena persisted, coiling herself around a lamp post. 'I didn't *do anything -*'

I said sorry (though I didn't mean it) and phoned a taxi. We sat in the gutter, retching like cuckoo clocks, and waited.

'I can't *believe* we got kicked out,' she said. 'This is such bullshit.'

'I know,' I said. 'Unbelievable.'

'I'm going to get this place shut down.' she said, a thick vein of phlegm blobbing down her chin. 'And get *him* sacked.' She emphasised 'him' with a viciousness that suggested she'd murder the bar manager's whole family should she ever find out where he lived.

Thankfully the taxi rolled up, its headlights like mustard powder in the dusk. We clambered inside and ignored the driver's warnings about cleaning fees and vomit, instead trying to make ourselves sick simply to inconvenience him.

'I can't do it,' bawled Sheena, tears in her eyes where she'd stuck her fingers down her throat. 'Nothing's coming up.'

I confessed I wasn't able to do so either, despite my deepest poking. Where was my gag reflex? 'You could make blowjob videos.' she laughed, slobbishly passing out against the windowpane.

Maybe I *could* make blowjob videos, I thought, resolving to get an application form tomorrow.

~

The driver shunted up outside our building. 'Out.' he

barked.

'Urgh,' said Sheena, spitting mouth dust onto the seats. 'I'll sleep here, thanks driver.'

'Me too.' I said, having inched into a serviceably comfortable position.

He thumped round to the passenger doors and flung them open. 'OUT.' he said, hauling us onto the gravel. We lay, unmoving, shivering and dizzy with drink.

'Bastard!' cried Sheena, waving her fists as he roared off into the cold, showering us in grit and pebbles.

We staggered to the door, too drunk to throw anything more than loose mints at the doorman. He offered no assistance whatsoever, watching us struggle to the lifts with a smile on his face.

We fell into the apartment and lurched to the fridge for cow meat. 'We should get that doorman sacked,' said Sheena, urinating into the kitchen bin. 'I'll make a complaint.' Why did she want everybody sacked?

I said nothing, mulching up smelly grey forkfuls.

CHAPTER 12

A week passed and we pattered nervously through the apartment, twiddling light switches and catching flies. We were acutely aware this could be our last week of freedom, yet couldn't enjoy it in the way I assumed imminent jailbirds were supposed to. We tried preparing meals unobtainable in prison: albumen hotpot, Bristolian water pork, egg and tuna loaves, but nothing brought us joy. Even news of Ed's ongoing coma ('a grumbling vegetable', according to Stu) failed to lift our spirits.

'Thank God his direct debit's still in place,' said Sheena. 'Otherwise we'd be in real trouble.'

She was right. For now we could still afford steamed fish heads without her having to return to work. It also meant we had collateral with which to bribe officials should we get locked up.

'Apparently prisoners get beaten with snake whips,' she said. 'Unless you give the guards money and handjobs. But even then there's no guarantee.'

Crumbs, I thought, only mildly aroused. I hoped I'd not get RSI from pleasuring randy jailers.

We languished in a throb of anxiety for days, unsure what awaited us in court. Hilary Bell had assured us there was nothing to worry about, but we dismissed his opinion as that of a predatory charlatan. 'He probably wants a handjob as well.' said Sheena, quite perceptively.

Friday dawned and we awoke, still drunk from the night before, and shared some pouched mackerel. Last night we'd returned to the Pig & Bucket and bribed the manager to grant Sheena access. As before, we spent an insulting amount on drinks and were ferried home by a furious taxi driver who demanded we pay for the cab windows we'd smashed. Sheena told him to get fucked, a wholly reasonable response that somehow enraged him further. He dropped us a mile from home, cursing our victimless horseplay and vowing to report us to Plod. We'd traipsed back, tipping over wheelie bins and barking wretchedly at rats.

We'd been instructed to dress smartly for our trial, as if judges cared a jot about such things. Given we'd done nothing wrong it seemed bizarre to fasten us into shirts and ties for the occasion. Nevertheless, we relented after Hilary Bell told us about a man who'd received life imprisonment for stealing a grapefruit simply because his pocket square was askew.

'That's nuts,' said Sheena, fetching a terylene overshirt. 'I'm not risking it.'

We booked a taxi to court and chuffed Thrushman's the whole way. The driver was encouraging, making embittered remarks about how nobody smoked real cigs anymore and that somehow this was the fault of immigration.

We alighted outside and were met by a skitter of photographers.

'This way.' said Hilary Bell, pulling us from the car like disgraced retail magnates. It was raining and he shielded us with an umbrella whose shaft was as thin as his arm. 'Don't say a word,' he said, as slimy press men lurched at us with tape recorders. 'It's a slow news day.'

Inside, we were led through squeaky corridors and seated on a bench outside a toilet. Hilary Bell scuttled around us like a mantis, talking into his phone and intermittently hissing with laughter. What was so funny? Surely our looming incarceration warranted nothing besides unassailable gloom?

'Why isn't he talking to *us?*' said Sheena, tearing at her nailskin. 'Shouldn't he be telling us what to say in there?'

'I don't know,' I said. 'Perhaps he thinks we'll get off.'

She considered this. 'Maybe you're right,' she said. 'We *are* innocent, after all. But why are the newspapers outside? It's not like we're high profile criminals. We're not media tycoons, for God's sake.'

'Could be a slow news day,' I said. 'That's what Hilary said.'

Sheena cocked a rueful eyebrow. 'Could be.' she said, implying she didn't believe this for a single second.

'Right,' said Hilary Bell, magnanimously finishing his phone call. 'Once we're in there, just sit down and say nothing, okay? Don't open your mouths. Everything's going to be fine.'

Before we could answer he was shuttling us into the courtroom and jamming us into our seats. I noticed several of the journalists from outside were leering from the gallery, presumably on the lookout for lies to print.

'This is weird,' Sheena whispered. 'Who are all these people?'

'Ignore them,' said Hilary Bell. 'Just rubberneckers. Happens at every trial.' I assumed he was right, though Sheena remained notably dubious. I didn't know what qualified her to question a law professional; perhaps she'd spent last night watching police procedurals and garnered the knowledge necessary to oversee a criminal prosecution.

'Remember, keep quiet.' said Hilary Bell, a pen cartwheeling between his long fingers. 'You'll be fine.'

A busybody arose and a hush befell the courtroom. 'All rise for the right honourable Lord Justice Wretchley.' he honked.

We exchanged a glance. That name.

Dressed in obstreperous judicial regalia, the moustachioed grandpa appeared before us, his quiet benevolence silencing even the cawing newspeople. He read aloud the particulars of the case, then invited the lawyers to present their motions. Hilary Bell was extraordinary, reasoning that our prosecution would deplete precious housing stock and force toddlers to live on rubbish tips. The jury was visibly sympathetic, with one member even dabbing her eye with a hanky. The prosecutor, by comparison, was laughable. He presented his case as if outlining a bad film treatment, peppering it with implausible caricatures and outlandish plot devices. The jury, now restless, was unimpressed, yawning loudly and fidgeting as he droned through our rap sheet.

Key witnesses were called: Stu, who assured the court we'd always been exemplary characters who acted with honour and integrity at all times, Handyman, who lied outright and claimed the gas leak had been a freak occurrence that couldn't possibly have been detected, and Muggins, the cafe owner, who provided a glowing character reference in spite of Sheena's desertion. I assumed this was because he didn't want the whereabouts of his wife discovered, for kidnapping carried hefty penalties unless committed by members of established rock bands.

The prosecution cross-examined the witnesses, a pointless exercise given Hilary Bell's powers of deception, and achieved nothing. Like a proud mafia family, nobody cracked. They all stuck rigidly to their stories, countering any contentious questions with 'I don't know what you're talking about.'

It was over in a matter of hours, at which point the jury retreated to their pen to hash out a decision. Hilary Bell flexed like a spider plant, evidently happy with the way it'd panned out. 'I think it's fair to say you're off the hook,' he said, his lips like sliced liver. 'Any questions?'

We shook our heads, unwilling to draw breath until the

verdict was handed down. He sipped nettle tea and ran a stringy hand over his notes. What had he written down? Sheena tried to steal a glance but he calmly closed the folder, implying it was none of her business. I stared about the courtroom and took note of the gawpers and ambulance chasers who'd turned out to watch us hang. They were a sorry gaggle of pondlife, all fussing with notepads and clingfilmed sandwiches, and I hoped they'd one day be hauled before a jury of morons, their liberty decided by a bedraggled cluster of halfwits.

'How long does this usually take?' said Sheena, trying not to shake. 'Any chance we could pop out for a couple of drinks?'

Hilary Bell shook his head. 'Unfortunately not,' he said. 'Need to do this by the book I'm afraid. Shouldn't be long now.'

I huffed my way through a calamitous machine coffee, horribly cobwebbed by last night's gin and cursing the treatment we'd received thus far. Heaven only knew what horrors awaited us in prison. Would they even have espresso machines? And would we have access to hand frothers? Sheena had advised the guards required frequent masturbatory relief, a service I hoped to leverage in exchange for cellblock privileges like microbeaded pillows and a nightly Tempranillo ration. Perhaps they had in place a loyalty system, I thought, whereby prisoners gave five handjobs a week and were awarded a free chisel or packet of cigs.

The room suddenly jabbered into life as the jury shambled back in looking intolerably pleased with themselves. It bordered on insulting, given their catalogue civvies and fat, feckless faces, that they'd been picked to decide our fates. Ideally I'd have been tried in a king's court by an assembly of corrupt sycophants who'd not only grant me a pardon, but also advocate strongly for my knighthood. Surveying the slovenly faces before me it seemed quite the opposite might transpire. Why would the court appoint such indolent slugs?

Lord Justice Wretchley, clearly having enjoyed several scotches during the recess, asked if they'd reached a verdict, to which the foreman, a snivelling toad in an immaculate club blazer, replied *yes, your honour*.

Sheena squeezed my hand like a Brannock device, her flesh warm and unnaturally swollen. This was the moment. Our precious freedom dangling like bribes before a councilman.

There was whispering in the gallery, quickly hushed by a thump of Wretchley's gavel. 'How do you find the accused?' he said.

'Not guilty, your honour.' said the juror.

'Hooray!' cried Sheena, quickly silenced by Hilary Bell.

Lord Wretchley ran through a few particulars before dismissing the case. I didn't know what to say. A line drawn under all our problems. We were free!

'I told you we were innocent!' crowed Sheena, clapping Hilary Bell so hard I thought he'd snap like a breadstick.

'Well done, great job,' he said, as if we'd lifted a finger to help our cause. 'Now let's get you outside. The press will want to hear your story.'

We emerged to a scuffle of microphones and questioning. *Do you feel this is an erosion of tenants' rights?* Absolutely not, we said. *Is this a victory for the private rented sector?* Of course. (Without the private rented sector people would spend their money on pitbulls and heroin.) *Are landlords subject to different laws than tenants?* We clarified that yes, tenants should be tried in paupers' court while landlords should be awarded state bonuses for their hard work accommodating those failed by the welfare system.

The reporters, all of whom seemed to represent right-wing hate rags, welcomed our comments with effusive nods and honks. We were barged and pawed as photographers jostled to secure saleable images.

'Thank you, thank you,' said Hilary Bell, bludgeoning us into a taxi. 'They'll be releasing a full statement in due course.'

The cab door slammed, and through the bluster we heard Hilary Bell shout that he'd see us at home. Would we *finally* be allowed to drink ourselves to death? Reading my thoughts, Sheena produced a bottle of mouthwash and bolted the lot. 'We've got a lot to celebrate.' she said, ignoring the cab driver's requests not to smoke.

'I really thought we were going to prison.' I said, with a lilt of disappointment. I'd actually begun acclimatising to the handjob idea and had been flexing accordingly.

'But we're not!' said Sheena. 'We're free!' She threw her head back like a shock victim and screamed to no one in particular.

The driver turfed us out at the quays road junction because we were jokingly trying to throttle him with seatbelts. 'We need to get him sacked,' said Sheena, retching into a flowerbed. 'Now we're free we can do anything we want. Imagine all the people we could get sacked!' She had a point. Without the nosy beak of Plod in our business we could lodge fabricated complaints against whomever we liked. We could try getting Ed sacked, I thought, wondering where in the future he worked.

The doorman greeted us with a craven smile, an obligation I imagined hurt more than all the mackerel tins we could throw at him. 'Good afternoon madam, good afternoon sir.' he said, as frostily as a commuter.

We tramped upstairs and collapsed on the balcony having hurled patio chairs at the neighbours' cars. We felt invulnerable; like we could act without penance or consequence, hospitalising anyone who stood in our way. I feared the doorman might soon meet such a fate.

CHAPTER 13

It was the eleventh, the date on which we'd decided to visit Lord Wretchley's mysterious club. Sheena had bought a new polo smock while I was resplendent in lambswool, fully deserving of praise and adulation for my modish garb.

'Don't we look wonderful?' said Sheena.

'Absolutely,' I said, adjusting my tie like a hedge fund criminal. 'I'd not be surprised if they lavish us with treasure and jewels.'

She nodded. 'We deserve it. Especially after that ridiculous trial. We deserve to be spoilt.'

Frustratingly, we'd been blacklisted by every cab firm in town, so had to pay the doorman two hundred pounds to drive us to the club in his hatchback. The only other option was the bus, a suggestion that caused Sheena to gag involuntarily. 'Why don't you just wheel me there in a portaloo?' she said, disgusted.

She was right. The bus was an utterly humiliating ordeal, made mostly unbearable by the commuters: all intolerable scum jostling for space among the luggage and crumbling pensioners. 'I'd rather go to a music festival.' she said, somewhat worryingly.

The doorman's car was spare and joyless, with worn seat fabric and grey plastic fixtures. The windows were handle-operated and the entertainment stretched to a cassette deck on which played speeches by communist figureheads. We sat in the back, forbidden from smoking and obligated not to strangle him while driving. 'So what *can* we do?' said Sheena, hilariously ungrateful for the lift. 'Can we spit on your neck?'

The doorman shook his head. Spit on his neck and we'd be walking to the club. We subsequently sulked, watching him mouth along to the speeches like a sentient dummy. He'd removed his doorman's hat, presumably so as not to appear too much like our chauffeur, and drove proudly, often relaxing his posture and closing his eyes like a free man. Suddenly Sheena clapped him on the shoulder, corrupting his dreams and eliciting a bark. 'What do you want?' he said.

'Can you drive us back as well?' she said, anticipating the evening's blackout. 'We can't get the bus. We just can't.'

Realising he was our only means of transportation he agreed, on the condition we pay him another two hundred pounds. 'Take it or leave it.' he said, as if he were donating rotten fruit to the homeless.

'Fine,' said Sheena. 'But you've got to wait for us outside.'

He agreed, reasoning he'd be better off sitting in a car than being pelted with sardine tins.

We rattled through Crumbford and hit traffic heading into Plugwood Lock. Buoyed by a snifter of methylated spirits, Sheena wound down her window and roared at the car in front, screaming at the driver to hit a lamp post. 'I'll spit on your grave!' she screeched, prompting sad reactionary honks.

'I'm sure he'll hit a lamp post soon.' I said, trying to sound reassuring. I was strangely nervous about the evening ahead, given how little we knew about where we were going. Lord Wretchley aside, we'd know nobody at the event. And how much did we even know about him? He'd clearly rigged our trial and freed us, but to what end?

I hoped we'd not end up specimens in a human zoo, dancing for the gratification of parliamentary backbenchers.

The building would've been unnoticeable had we not had a map. The evening was cold and we eased gingerly down a narrow, unlit backstreet running parallel to a canal; dark in the shadow of industrial frontage. The buildings were neither residential nor commercial, rather they were disused municipal centres and boarded-up warehouses, presumably used by infantilised men as places to fight.

'Stop, Doorman,' said Sheena. 'This is the place.'

He crunched to a halt and we slid out, less rambunctiously than usual. There was something oppressive about the freezing air and dense, unbroken darkness that kept us from breaking windows and whooping. Instead we clanked down a flight of steps and found a corrugated black door, invisible from street level, guarded by Birmingham bars and a dull steel intercom.

'What do we do?' I said, my finger dithering over the button.

'I don't know,' said Sheena. 'Press it I suppose.'

I depressed it, causing a shrill ring. We stood in the doorway, freezing and parched, hoping we'd be permitted access.

'I'd love a whisky,' whispered Sheena. 'Do you think they'll have whisky?'

'I hope so,' I whispered back. 'I'd quite like to get shitfaced.'

'Me too.' she said, despite having been shitfaced for the last six months.

The intercom crackled and we stiffened (not due to arousal). 'Yes?' it said. We stammered back our names.

'I should've brought a cardigan.' said Sheena, her breath cloudy in the cold.

'Sorry?' said the intercom. 'What was that?'

'Nothing,' said Sheena. 'I was just saying that I should've brought a cardigan. Because of the cold.'

'Not to worry,' said the voice. 'It's lovely and warm in here.'

We looked at each other.

'Can we come in?' I said.

'Of course, just give me a minute.' it said, keeningly polite.

'Also, have you got any whisky?' she Sheena.

I burrowed my hands into my pockets and tensed my jaw. The intercom was silent. She shrugged. Maybe we'd pushed our luck.

'Sorry about that,' came the voice. 'Bloody paperwork. You understand.'

The buzzer rasped and the door unlatched. It weighed more than a bailiff and took two of us to thrust open. Inside was black and smelled of iron and chemicals. We strode into the darkness. The floor was carpeted in matted wicker and was warm despite the temperature outside. 'Probably burning witches.' said Sheena, perceptive as ever.

There was a dim, custard-coloured glow at the end of the passage and we tottered towards it. We turned the corner and arrived at a foreboding iron door, above which was mounted an ornate light fixture.

'Should we knock?' I said, my breath swirling in the light. How many more doors would there be?

'Christ, I suppose so,' said Sheena. 'It's like trying to get into a fucking A&E department.'

We clanged on the door, more effusively than before. No reply. We waited. One minute. Two minutes.

'For God's sake,' said Sheena, her temper ragged and threadbare. 'I'm so thirsty. Should we just get Doorman to drive us to the Pig & Bucket? At least there we can get through the *door*.'

Three minutes. Three-and-a-half minutes.

'Maybe that's a good idea,' I said. 'We've been waiting here for hours.'

'Exactly,' said Sheena. 'They obviously think we're mugs.'

Once it reached four minutes we gave up, reasoning the whole operation had been a waste of time.

'They can't keep us waiting like junkies,' said Sheena. 'We deserve respect. We've worked so hard to get here.'

I concurred, mildly aggrieved there hadn't been a welcoming party greeting us with palm fronds and moonflower garlands. Were we held in such low esteem?

We were heading back up the passageway when we heard a metallic *screech*.

'Where the hell are you two going?' came a voice. It was familiar, comforting. 'For heaven's sake get yourselves in here.' It was Lord Wretchley, poised in the doorway with an ascot tie and a port and lemon in hand. 'Sorry for the wait,' he said. 'Bloody security. God knows what they do all day. Eat chips I imagine. Bloody shambles.'

Only slightly disappointed that we'd not be drinking ourselves senseless at the Pig & Bucket, we accepted his embrace and headed inside. He smelled of horsehair and was lightly perspiring, giving him the appearance of a freshly glazed ham. 'Follow me, won't you.' he said, his port sloshing precariously in its tumbler. 'Sorry it's a bit of a labyrinth. Planning permission, you know.'

Neither of us had any idea what he meant, yet we cooed and nodded as if we'd held positions of authority on nationwide planning committees.

'You must be bloody parched,' he said, reading our minds like a sideshow fraud. 'Let's get you something to drink, shall we?'

Sheena elbowed me excitedly, clearly thrilled she'd soon be able to satiate her rampant thirst.

He led us into a large, low-ceilinged bunker room, foggy with cigar smoke and club collars. There were men everywhere: paunched and doughy, bespectacled and thin, ruddy-cheeked and jowly, all guzzling port and laughing like demons. Would they eat us? Make us fight?

'Follow me, friends,' said Wretchley, gesticulating theatrically. He had a thespian air about him, a tactile nature that suggested he'd happily molested stagehands in provincial dressing rooms. 'Let's get you something strong!'

We jostled through the chattering mass, overhearing gobbets of conversation ('...*I bankrupted her family after she reported me...*'), eventually arriving at a long black bar.

'Look at *that*.' whispered Sheena with a reverent hush. She nodded at the back bar, displayed on which were innumerable bottles, everything from Libyan frog tonic to absinthe drained from extracted peasant livers.

'Good evening.' said the bar boy, a waistcoated model with bruises on his face and a dog collar around his neck.

'Get them anything they want,' said Wretchley. He waved at us. 'They're our guests.'

The boy looked at us. He had palm marks on his cheeks. Was he a sex slave? 'Okay,' he said, spiky and clipped. 'What would you like?'

Sheena surveyed the bottles, twinkling like crystal towers, celestial and rich with promise. 'What's that one?' she said, jabbing at an oversized glass bollock.

'That's Warpecker,' he said. 'It's a glandular love whisky.'

'Sounds mad,' said Sheena. 'Can we have that?'

The boy looked to Wretchley for approval.

'Anything they want,' he said, waving a ringmasterly hand and splashing his drink on the boy's waistcoat. 'Blowjobs, whatever. Just make sure they're looked after.'

The boy didn't blink, his eyes glassy and inscrutable. He set down the bottle and presented us two glasses. 'Enjoy.' he said, with all the humourlessness of a men's rights activist.

The drink felt blobby in our mouths, like coagulated gravy or refrigerated semen. Still, it was immensely strong and gifted us an immediate and rapacious buzz.

'Crumbs,' I said. 'That's bananas.'

'Yes it is,' said Sheena, her face blotched red like a ski mask. 'Let's finish it.'

We drank like footballers, making an admirable dent in the whisky while acclimatising to our fabulous new lair. The room was tastefully sparse, minimally decorated with credit cards littering the floor. There were tables in the corners but the patrons all stood, presumably too drugged and sloshed to sit still for a single second. They were a spirited group, boisterous and generally out for a harmless night of fun. They were absolutely our kind of people.

'Good to see *you two* again!' came a sudden voice. We cut short our discussion on beheadings to find fleshy hands on our shoulders. 'I think you owe me a drink!'

It was the juror from the trial, he who'd delivered our Not Guilty verdict.

'What are you doing here?' said Sheena, deliberately blowing Thrushman's smoke in his face. 'Shouldn't you be off counting beans or whatever?'

He laughed breathlessly, suggesting some constriction of the bronchus. 'No, no, no,' he said. 'I'm a friend of Horton's. You know, Lord Wretchley? I do a lot of his trials, you see. He likes a familiar face in the courtroom.'

'Oh, yes. Yes, of course,' I said, impressed by his brassnecked corruptibility. I poured the drinks and we toasted new friendships.

'So you two are landlords,' he said. 'How many properties?'

Sheena paused. 'Only two,' she said, a great sadness in her voice. 'And we live in one of them.'

He looked at us with an expression reserved for widowers and comic book collectors. 'Wow,' he said, his heart pouring sympathy. 'I'm so sorry guys, I had no idea.'

'That's okay,' she said. 'You weren't to know.'

She wiped her eyes. Was she crying? 'It's just the smoke,' she said, lying of course. She continued, her voice wavering: 'I mean, we did want a third place, but we had to do a load of repairs, then this trial got in the way, you know how it is.'

The juror pursed his lips solemnly. 'I understand,' he

said. 'Things get in the way. It's not your fault.' He poured another round and withdrew a phone from his pocket. 'Tell you what,' he said. 'I might be able to help you out.'

'What do you mean?' I said. 'Help us out how?'

He handed me the phone. On the screen was a photo of a building; what looked like a small block of flats.

'What's this?' said Sheena. 'A paedophile safehouse?'

'Haha, no,' he laughed. 'Not even *I* know where those are. No, this is a building I own. Plugwood Lock development, three flats, not a bad little income.'

'Looks lovely.' I said. (It looked like a Gulag outbuilding.)

'But why are you showing it to us?' said Sheena, lighting two Thrushman's. She'd grown receptive to the juror during our conversation, especially since he'd revealed himself as more than just a court-appointed shill. What *was* his game?

'I'm having a bit of trouble managing the place,' he said. 'The rest of my properties, the jury work, it takes up a lot of my time. You see the problem?'

Yes, yes, of course, we said, now unapologetically eating out of his hand.

'So I'm going to need to get rid of it, you see. And I was wondering-' he gestured at us with his glass, 'if maybe you'd like to take it on?'

We said nothing, our breath held firm.

He continued: 'obviously there'd be a discount - we're all friends here after all - and I'd much prefer to keep it in the club.'

I glugged down my drink and reached for the bottle but it was empty. I felt an overwhelming urge to get as drunk as humanly possible.

'What kind of discount are you talking about?' said Sheena, admirably retaining her composure.

'Oh we don't need to go into all that now,' said the juror. 'But I think something around the fifty percent mark is reasonable, don't you?'

'Fifty percent?' she gasped. 'As in, *half price?*'

He waved over the bar boy. 'Another round when you're ready, young man.'

Sheena stared at me, mouthing the words *half price?* in a manner she must've thought subtle.

'Well it doesn't make any sense pricing you out now, does it?' he said. 'And besides, you'll probably end up selling it back to me in a few years.'

'Oh, what? Really?' she said, rightly unnerved at the thought of an insecure property portfolio.

'Haha, don't worry,' he said, handing us our drinks. 'That's just the way it works here. See him over there?' he pointed across the room to a bespectacled stickman whose nose was powdered with cocaine. 'That's the health secretary.'

I squinted through the smoke. 'Do you mean,' I said, sounding distinctly like a thickie, 'the government health secretary?'

'Haha, yes, that's the one.' he said.

I looked again: the health secretary was chewing up banknotes and spitting the pulp into people's' drinks.

'He sold me these flats about six months ago. Well, not *sold* exactly. He gave them to me in exchange for a basement I own in Crumbford. Good little place actually. Soundproofed, police monitored, the lot. Great if you've got a sex ring you want to keep quiet. Are you two into that kind of thing?'

Mechanically we shook our heads, having never been asked such a question.

'Well, he's the man to speak to if you're ever curious. He does all sorts. Not sure what's *en vogue* at the moment, although I did hear something about kidnapping vulnerables. Apparently that's all the rage right now.'

'Oh right,' I said, nodding tacitly as I scanned the room and noticed we were the most vulnerable people here.

'Well he's not kidnapping us,' said Sheena. 'I'll bury him if he tries anything.'

The juror ran a hand through his hair. 'God, listen to us,' he said. 'All doom and gloom. Why don't we change the subject? Have a toast?' he waved again at the bar boy, who was wistfully tweezing stray hairs. 'A round of Warpeckers over here,' he said. Then to us: 'so thrilled to have met you both.'

We toasted our friendship (again) and pressed on with the laudable task of drinking ourselves into a semi-conscious netherworld where propriety and compassion were cast squarely in the mud. As the evening tore on we edged further into the throng, snorting high-grade cocaine with the health secretary and enjoying his stories about everyday ministerial corruption ('...*I submitted an expense claim for homeless pornography - no one batted an eyelid...*').

We were introduced around at a dizzying rate: backbenchers, bankers, board directors, CEOs, CFOs, COOs, all of whom cocked their heads in sympathy when we mentioned our meagre two properties. One reveller even asked us to repeat ourselves, mistakenly assuming we'd said *too many* properties, seemingly a genuine concern among the members given how many of them tried to offload on us their surplus assets. 'Houses are just *cumbersome*, aren't they?' they said, explaining how there was only so many tenants you could sell into slavery before the families came knocking.

The evening spun on; a rampage of Champers and parliamentary drugs, until we found ourselves slumped on a corner table trying valiantly to chuff cigs but without the requisite lung capacity.

'What time is it?' moaned Sheena. 'Is it still nighttime?'

I hadn't a clue; there were no windows in the club and the street level exit was barred by an iron door. Neither of us had a watch and our phones had long since puttered out. 'I'll go and ask someone.' I said, wheezing from passive smoke inhalation.

I rose and steadied myself on a wall-mounted jockstrap. I was tortuously drunk but the cocaine had temporarily suppressed the effects of the alcohol, leaving me incapacitated but still vaguely lucid. I stumbled into the throng, now thinned out after hours of indulgence, and mumbled questions about the time. I was clearly more sozzled than I'd thought, for I was either ignored or openly laughed at. I spotted the health secretary at the bar; he'd urinated into a glass and was offering the bar boy money to drink it.

'Do you know the time?' I said, slurring beyond all comprehension.

'He's going to do it!' he said, jabbing a sinewy finger at the boy. 'Watch!'

It was then I noticed a shaft of light at the far end of the bar, the crack of a door that'd been left ajar. I approached it and pawed it open. Inside was weathered and mucky like a high street stockroom; there were overalls and wire cords hanging from the walls and stacked crates filled with chemicals. Before I could steal anything Wretchley appeared, seemingly from a cupboard, swinging a bucket and whistling the national anthem.

'Hi,' I said, drooling and flushed. 'Do you know the time?'

'Oh - hello old chap,' he said, almost imperceptibly riled. 'You look a little spangled. Are you feeling okay? Let's clear out of here, shall we? Give the staff some space.'

He set down the bucket and I noticed it was half-filled with compost scraps.

'Do you know the time?' I said again, my head spinning like a football ratchet.

He checked his watch. 'It's nine-thirty,' he said. 'Time for a cigar, I think.'

We exited back to the bar and I returned to our table. 'It's only nine-thirty,' I said. 'Still early.'

'Nine-thirty?' said Sheena, courageously trying to smoke three cigs. 'In the morning?'

I hesitated. Naturally I'd assumed he'd meant nine-thirty in the evening, but that'd suggest we'd only been here for a few hours. Was it really nine-thirty in the morning? 'I'll go and ask.' I said, again stumbling to the bar.

Lord Wretchley was reclining with his cigar, sucking it like sternum marrow.

'Hi,' I said. 'Is it the evening?'

He sipped a port and lemon and eyed me keenly. 'Haha, no dear boy. It's morning now, old chap.'

Dumbfounded, I clattered back to Sheena to report my findings.

'I think we should go home,' she said. 'Doorman should still be outside.'

'Yes.' I said. My head felt like a deodorant stick, gummy and dense with chemicals, and I needed to breathe clean oxygen.

We rose and thanked Lord Wretchley for his hospitality, though I imagine our compliments came out as slobbering slurs.

'So wonderful to have you both tonight,' he said, bidding us farewell with a plummy handshake. 'Come back again soon.'

The health secretary was collapsed on the floor with the bar boy, cradling his penis like a milked pig. We stepped over him on the way out, pocketing handfuls of banknotes he'd left scattered nearby. We returned up the passage, now brighter but still mostly shielded from the daylight. It was deeply disconcerting being so drunk at so civilised an hour, especially given we were fizzing with cocaine and unprepared for even a minute of sleep. We exited into oppressive sunshine and Sheena screamed like a penetrated fox. 'It's too bright!' she said. 'Get me home!'

I looked up and down the street, searching for the doorman's nasty little car. I half assumed he'd driven into the canal, drowning himself and ending his torment once and for all. With a prod of disappointment I then spotted it, its coathanger aerial flailing pathetically in the breeze.

We approached and noticed he'd lowered the driver's seat and was lying horizontal with his eyes closed, an unprecedented oasis of calm in an ongoing life of humiliation.

'Wake up, Doorman!' yelled Sheena, hammering on the glass. 'Take us home!'

He snapped awake and wound down the window. 'I still need another two hundred pounds,' he said. 'Otherwise you're not going anywhere.'

Begrudgingly we acquiesced, agreeing to stop at a cash machine on the way home. Despite this, Sheena floated the idea of strangling him and driving ourselves back.

'Why not?' she said, struggling to remain upright in the back seat. 'No one would miss him. Poxy doorman.'

She was trying to whisper but was practically shouting, disparaging and insulting him right to his face. 'He'd probably enjoy it,' she said. 'Everyone likes being strangled.'

Rather than try quietening her (impossible) I looked out of the window at the passing wasteland, drooling on my lambswool and failing to finish cigs. I'd light them, hack down several puffs, then defeatedly stub them out on Doorman's upholstery. I felt weak and spooked, zapped and exhausted, like a washing line groaning under the weight of denim and wet towels.

Doorman remained silent, ignoring Sheena's increasingly vicious insults (...*a worthless slug...standing in the lobby, wanking all day*...) and driving with the meditative calm of a prisoner condemned to death.

We arrived home and spat on his car by way of thanks. We hauled ourselves upstairs and crashed out on the floor, our hearts palpitating and our heads spinning in infinite, dizzying corkscrews. It'd been a success. We were in the club.

CHAPTER 14

I awoke on the bedroom floor after several hours of fitful unconsciousness. It wasn't sleep, more a brief bout of restless thrashing during which I'd soiled myself and endured a nightmare about having a full-time job.

My head felt impassably clogged, like every duct was thick with slime and every nerve feathered by hairdressing scissors. I gobbled a whole packet of painkillers, hoping they'd hospitalise me and thus provide access to intravenous hydration. Predictably, I remained conscious and staggered to the kitchen for water. I took a sip and immediately vomited it back into the sink. Clearly I'd need more than a boiled egg and an espresso to get over this.

I shuffled to the balcony, hoping fresh air might revitalise me. It was bright and cold, similar to the day Grandma had tortured my sister's favourite frog, and I took deep, restorative breaths. I looked around for the doorman, hoping to unwind by throwing soapstones at his head, but he was absent from his post. How irresponsible, I thought, concerned for the unguarded lobby. Who'd protect the shrubbery in his absence?

I dug into my pockets for Thrushman's and unexpectedly retrieved a bundle of banknotes, all spattered and limp, equating to nearly a thousand pounds. Probably a gift from Lord Wretchley, I thought, money to spend on club blazers and monk strap brogues. At last we were receiving honest, decent remuneration for our hard work: financial perks befitting our diligence and ingenuity.

Sheena groaned; she'd slept on the kitchen floor and was in twice as much pain than if she'd slept in bed. She crawled towards me and hoisted herself upright using a balcony chair. 'I can't breathe.' she said, wheezing horribly. Her nose was red and cornflaked with dead skin, while her eyes were dry and dead like insectoid food balls. 'Have you got a cig?'

We lit Thrushmans and she wheezed like a gypsy's accordion.

'My head feels like a smashed crab.' she said.

'Would you like a whisky?' I said, selflessly casting aside my own agony.

'I don't think I could stomach it,' she said. 'I can barely finish this cig.'

It was then I knew she must be really suffering, for I'd never once known her to turn down a soothing breakfast whisky. In an effort to rouse her, and knowing how much she loved money, I retrieved the wedge of banknotes and presented them to her.

'Where did you get *that?*' she said, her eyes regaining their sparkle.

'I don't know,' I said. 'I think Wretchley might've given it to us.'

'Makes sense,' she said. 'We deserve it for all our hard work.'

We spent the day coiled on the sofas, watching televised baking and chundering into buckets when necessary.

'When is this going to end?' said Sheena, dragging her palms over her face. 'I feel *so* ill.'

'Me too,' I said. 'Maybe we should spend this money to cheer ourselves up?'

'Yes, maybe we should,' she said, smiling meekly.

We found a restaurant that delivered Brazilian lobster

tails and Piedmont truffles and proceeded to blow every penny of our earnings on dinner. Prior to our windfall it would've been prohibitively expensive but now we ordered with abandon, adding ludicrously expensive side dishes and ostentatious puddings to the order. We even spaffed a hundred pounds on a premium delivery slot.

'Money well spent.' said Sheena, easing into her fifth brandy of the day.

Our dinner was a riot of crustacean shell and dense fungus, roman grapes and calf butter that we wolfed down with the voracity of liberated detainees.

Once the last puck of lobster meat was gone, we lay back, exhausted, and sponged garlic fluid from our foreheads.

'We should be eating that every day,' said Sheena. 'Why have we been messing about with cow meat?'

'I don't know,' I said. 'I suppose it seemed like an unnecessary expense.'

She agreed. Food had never been factored into our drink budget, as its inclusion was inversely proportional to the intoxication levels achievable through alcohol. 'If you stuff yourself full of chips you don't get as wrecked,' she said. 'Simple as that.'

I rose, scooped up the sodden food containers and headed to the bin.

'What are you doing?' she said. 'Shouldn't we be throwing that at the doorman's head?'

'Of course,' I said. 'Sorry, my head's still thumping.'

We headed to the balcony clutching artisanal tubs and foil food platters. I was already prising them into throwable spheres, hoping my hangover wouldn't detrimentally affect my aim.

'Where is he?' said Sheena. 'Is he hiding?'

I scanned the car park, the building entrance, the dockside. No Doorman.

'His car's not there either,' she said, pointing to his parking space. 'Maybe he's killed himself.'

'Maybe he's got the day off.' I said.

'But who'll stop the burglars?' she said, furrowed with concern. 'And the squatters? And the prospective buyer viewings?'

I winced. 'Shall we go down and look for him?'

'Yes,' she said anxiously. 'Let's go now.'

~

The lobby was silent. The shrubs stood undisturbed against the windows, proud and upright like sentries, enforcing security in Doorman's absence.

'Hello?' said Sheena.

'Doorman?' I echoed. I wondered if he had a name (though I'm sure I wouldn't bother using it if he did).

'Is anyone here?' said Sheena.

We looked at each other. What was going on? I edged towards the reception desk: a wooden platform on which were positioned sharded vases and a leather blotter. There was no evidence of his presence: no hat, no jacket, no communist pamphlets. Had he been beaten senseless by the far right?

'Look.' said Sheena. She pointed to a list of contacts taped to the rearside of the desk.

'Facilities Management,' I read. 'Maybe we should call them. Find out what's going on.'

'Alright,' said Sheena. 'You do it. I'm too hungover.'

I dialled the number and fiddled with the phone cord.

'Hello, FM,' came a voice. It was a woman who sounded like an SS dignitary. 'Which site are you calling from?'

'Which what?' I said.

'Site. Which site. Which *building* are you calling from?'

'Oh,' I said. 'Drillfield Quays. The one by the harbour.'

'Good.' she said. 'Is that Roy Foggins?'

'What?' I said. 'Who's Roy Foggins?'

'Mr. Foggins is the security supervisor at that site,' she

said. 'The doorman.'

'Oh,' I said. 'No, no, he's not here. That's why I'm phoning. We live in the building and we were wondering where he was.'

The SS dignitary paused, possibly noting something down. 'You're saying Mr. Foggins hasn't arrived for work today?' she said. 'That the site's unsupervised?'

'Well, yes, I suppose so,' I said. 'There's nobody here to guard us.'

'Right, thank you. Thank you for reporting it. We'll contact Mr. Foggins and launch an investigation immediately.'

She disconnected abruptly and I wondered what might happen to Doorman.

'They'll probably just take away his coffee pot,' said Sheena, skirting back to the lift. 'Nothing to worry about.'

~

Several days later we learnt Doorman had been sacked with immediate effect. His firm cited gross misconduct, binning him without bonus or redundancy pay, even requesting he return his uniform so as not to tarnish their brand with failure. He'd protested, insisting he'd been tired after ferrying us around all night, a claim his bosses dismissed as the ramblings of a skiver.

'Serves him right,' said Sheena, with little conviction.

We were leaning over the balcony throwing rubbish at neighbours' cars, though it brought little joy. If only Doorman were down there, I thought, daydreaming of knocking his hat off with an expired spam tin.

'I wonder if he'll get another job,' I said. 'Or maybe start a doorperson recruitment agency.'

'Yeah, right,' she sneered. 'Chances are he'll kill himself. That's what I'd do.'

I hoped he wouldn't but couldn't rule it out. He was a withdrawn middle-aged communist without looks or means; surely the best he could hope for was a dismal houseshare in Crumbford with a cluster of rent slaves who ate disreputable curries and resented feminism.

'If he's struggling we could rent him one of our flats,' said Sheena. 'Once that juror hands over the deeds, we'll have three of them.'

'That's a good idea,' I said. 'He could be the doorman. Keep the place safe.'

'Good thinking,' she said. 'We'll need a doorman. Make sure it's not burglarised.'

'He might not even be struggling at all though,' I said. 'He might've bought a five-bedroom townhouse in the sixties when they cost nothing.'

'Yes, maybe.' said Sheena.

~

It transpired Doorman didn't live in swinging opulence, and was instead struggling more than we could've ever imagined. We met him one evening as we were leaving the building, both excited for a session at the club, while he was visiting to collect some personal effects. His eyes were shaded by a military-green cloth cap and he wore a bomber jacket seemingly salvaged from a public clothing repository.

'Madam. Sir.' he said, his eyes fixed firmly on the ground.

'Oh hi.' we said, sheepishly. Why did we feel so bad?

'Just picking up a few things,' he mumbled. 'Diaries and so forth.'

We hadn't the heart to tell him his locker had been cleared out and his possessions thrown in a skip a week ago.

'Oh, okay.' we said.

'How're you doing?' said Sheena, indecorously lucid after half a bottle of port. 'Are you working?'

'I'm fine.' he said, hurrying off. His tattered shoes

suggested he wasn't remotely fine.

'Do you need a place to live?' she blurted.

'What?' he said, turning back nervously. 'What do you mean?'

'We've just bought some flats,' she said. 'You could rent one if you wanted.'

He paused. 'How much?'

We dithered, having not yet discussed it in that much detail.

'Maybe we could make a deal,' she said. 'Maybe you could be our -' she paused, presumably not wanting to use the word *servant*. 'Our caretaker.'

We hashed out the details right there in the lobby: it was agreed he'd pay us minimal rent in exchange for maintaining the building; keeping the tenants quiet, liaising with Stu and - most vitally - ensuring we weren't ever bothered with such trivialities.

'We don't want to hear a thing about it,' said Sheena. 'Stu, the tenants, anyone, they all go through you, understand? For all they know we live on the moon.'

'Alright,' he said. 'I'm in.'

~

Astonishingly he drove us to the club, his manner genial and less frosty than before. He accepted Sheena's offer of a swig of port, he lit a cig, he even blasted out a lecture on land redistribution at top volume.

I advised we stop at a cash machine to pay him his driver's fee but he dismissed the idea, insisting we'd helped him enough already today.

'More money to light cigars with.' laughed Sheena,

He explained how our accumulation of property jarred with his personal politics, but also recognised his need for shelter and employment, two necessities the state wouldn't automatically provide. 'I live above a tuna merchants,' he said. 'In a utility cupboard. I use j-cloths for warmth.'

'That's awful,' I said, barely listening. 'I'm sure the new place will be better.'

'It has to be,' he said. 'Anything's better than sleeping on a sackful of fish guts.'

We rolled up outside the club and left the doorman outside, happily chaining cigs and waving us inside like a friend might do.

'That was a good thing to do,' I said. 'We're really nice people.'

'We're amazing,' said Sheena, clanging down the metal stairs. 'I can't believe how lovely we are.'

We were buzzed in without even a cursory namecheck, so familiar were we at the club nowadays. We'd since learnt it was called the Ten Hours Club, something kept secret from new and untrusted members, and was named after the Ten Hours act, legislation that restricted the working hours of women and children in textile mills to a paltry ten hours a day, a law the founding members had dedicated their lives to overturning.

Inside was characteristically dark and we found Lord Wretchley at the bar discussing brogues with the health secretary. 'No brown in town, old sock, that's the rule. Most unseemly.' He was referring to a tradition whereby men wore black brogues during the week and brown at the weekend, when they'd escape the city to the seclusion of the English countryside.

'Bloody sensible,' said the health secretary, adjusting his hornrims. 'God knows I've seen some shockers recently. Espadrilles and all sorts.'

'Madness.' said Wretchley.

We ordered a bottle of Warpecker and eased in beside them, lighting Thrushmans and flicking ash on the bar boy's waistcoat.

'Hello you two,' said Wretchley with a conspiratorial wink. He hugged us and tickled our cheeks with his moustache. 'Fabulous to see you both.'

We greeted him and, as usual, toasted to success.

'Is the juror here?' said Sheena. 'We need to talk to him about those flats.'

'Oh God,' said the health secretary, sympathetically clapping me on the shoulder. 'Heard about your situation, old chap. Only got the two properties, eh? Rotten luck.'

'I know,' said Sheena, welling up when reminded of our meagre assets. 'But we'll be okay. We've got a deal in the pipeline.'

'Ah-ha! The Plugwood Lock flats,' he said. 'Yes, I heard about that. Great little investment. Tenants are a bloody pain though. But I'm sure you can up the rent, price them out. Or, knowing you two, just blow them up. Hahaha!' We guffawed at Ed's hospitalisation and made explosion noises between laughs.

'How is he, your tenant?' said Wretchley. 'What's his name, something Greene -'

'He's in a coma,' said Sheena. 'No idea when he'll wake up.'

'As long as he keeps paying rent,' I said. 'We don't really care.'

'That's the spirit,' said the health secretary. 'These bloody renters, what a waste of space, eh? Why don't they just buy their own bloody property?'

We nodded sombrely at the inconvenience presented by tenants. Sheena even mock-spat at the floor at the very mention of them.

'Never rented a house in my life,' continued the health secretary. 'Makes no sense.'

'Neither have we.' Sheena lied quickly. Clearly it'd be foolish to mention our previous entanglement with Gadswood's Estates, the most ruthless and litigious lettings agent in the country.

'Absolutely not,' I said. 'Renting's for idiots.'

'Bloody well is,' said the health secretary. 'If anything, there's *too many* houses on the market. If these renters pulled their socks up, they could buy at least two or three properties each.'

The bar boy, evidently a renter himself (poor fool), was clenching his jaw and clutching a glass so hard I thought it'd smash into a million pieces in his hands.

'Oh look, here's our friend,' said Wretchley, tapping cigar ash on the bar boy's sleeve. He gestured across the room to where the juror was piping cocaine up his nose, laughing recklessly at a story about migrant camps ('...*I never thought a machine gun would be such fun...*'). He saw us and roared over, thrillingly wired.

'How are you, old sock?' said Wretchley, pouring him a Warpecker.

'Bloody great, old man,' he said. 'Just been blething about one of these camps that's been closed down. Terrible business.'

'Who wants to go camping in this weather?' said the health secretary. 'Stay in a bloody hotel, that's what I'd do.' Noting the juror's chalky-white nose he withdrew a wrap of cocaine from his pocket and vacuumed up a fortifying nostrilful. 'Ooft, I needed that.' he said.

'You're a mad thing,' said Wretchley, brushing residual cocaine from his nose with a handkerchief. 'Too much of that stuff will do you in, old chap.'

'Have you got a minute?' said Sheena to the juror. 'We wanted to talk about those flats you mentioned.'

'Ah, of course!' he said, flinging back his drink. 'Got the deeds right here. Have you got a pen? Seems I left mine downstairs.'

'Downstairs?' said Sheena. 'I didn't know there was a downstairs.'

Lord Wretchley jumped in: 'I'm sure he means downstairs at the courthouse, don't you, old thing?'

'Of course, of course, at the courthouse,' said the juror. 'Downstairs at the courthouse. That's what I meant.'

Why were they being so cagey? Surely it wasn't uncommon for a bar to have a downstairs area, to store beer barrels and suchlike?

'Here's a pen,' said Sheena, gently exasperated by their

indecisive goosing.

'Perfect,' said the juror, and plucked a stapling of papers from his blazer pocket. 'Just need you to sign here, and here, and we're done. The place is yours.'

'But what about the cost?' she said. 'We haven't paid you yet.'

'Oh pfft,' he said. 'Pay me whenever you like. Payday or whenever.' (Did he still think us wage slaves?)

We signed and passed him back the papers.

'Smashing,' he said, raising another of many toasts. 'To success!'

As had become customary, we drank Warpecker and gorged ourselves on nutrifying cocaine until the next morning, when we emerged, bolshy and fizzing, into the frosty yellow sunlight.

Doorman was sleeping in his car with the window ajar, like a dog, and we clambered into the back seat. 'Fancy a bite?' he said, holding out a carton of pig biscuits. Evidently he'd squirrelled away provisions for the night's lull.

'Absolutely not.' said Sheena, lighting two Thrushman's.

'No thanks,' I said, lighting three.

He too lit a cig and we rattled off like homecoming soldiers.

CHAPTER 15

The new flats were appalling. Worse, arguably, than the place we'd rented Ed. There were three residences, boxed atop each other like packing crates, each costing two thousand pounds a month in rent.

'We'll get that increased,' said Sheena, leafing through the inventories. 'At that price they're ripping *us* off.'

'Absolutely,' I said. 'It's not a homeless shelter, after all.'

From the outside the walls were sloppily pebbledashed and ran green with mould, while the windowframes were splintered and bowed with neglect. There were no visible curtains, only newspapers, parcel tape and rags hanging limply like laddered tights.

We entered the hallway and were immediately spattered by moisture. It was condensation, plopping from the ceiling like a sapping tree.

'What's that smell?' said Sheena, huffing on her inhaler. 'Smells familiar.'

'I think it's damp.' I said, running a finger through the furry black slime.

'Bloody tenants,' she said. 'Can't take care of anything. Why don't they clean this place up?'

I know, it's awful, I said.

'Are all three flats occupied?' she said, leafing through

the documents. 'If so, we're going to need to kick someone out. Doorman needs somewhere to stay.'

'Looks like it,' I said, noting the three postboxes. The post itself comprised mostly crinkly envelopes and final payment demands, all floppy from airborne moisture.

'We can bin that lot,' she said absentmindedly, still poring over the documents. 'Yep, we'll definitely need to kick someone out. Who's it going to be?'

She presented me with details of the tenants: on the top floor was a particularly elderly woman who, given her age, was surely close to death.

'No use kicking her out,' said Sheena. 'She'll die soon anyway. Don't want her family kicking up a stink.'

In the middle flat were two student girls, both addled and reckless according to the notes. 'They should stay.' said Sheena.

'Why?' I said. 'Can't we just turf them out and burn their possessions?' (I'd cohabited with students several years prior and they'd very deliberately tried to ruin my life. I was thus naturally predisposed to wish only the very worst for them.)

'They're scum, obviously,' she said, 'but look at their direct debits.' She pointed to the page. 'Their parents pay their rent. That means we don't need to worry about them falling behind with payments, or spending their rent money on Fentanyl.'

I admired her calculated ruthlessness. For Sheena it was only about money, and having money meant she could afford to drink herself blind without worrying about getting up for work the next day.

On the ground floor were two men, in their mid-thirties, who worked in recruitment and tax collection.

'Obviously we get rid of them,' she said. 'No doubt about it.'

'I agree.' I said, not really knowing why.

'Best to have Doorman living on the ground floor,' she said. 'He can act as gatekeeper. Keep the rest of them in line.'

'Also it'd be nice to see a tax collector out on the street,' I said. 'It'd serve him right.'

'Yes it would.' she said.

The place was so dank and filthy we didn't bother staying to meet the tenants, instead instructing Doorman to evict the men on the ground floor and advise them we'd be keeping all of their deposits. (Lord Wretchley had confirmed he'd dismiss any claim they made to recoup the money.)

'It's only fair,' said Sheena, wheezing like a piston. 'Look at the mess they've made of our hallway.'

~

We were in Muggins Cafe, gnawing cow meat and jellied hen, when Doorman arrived. He sat down and lit a cig (he smoked Balkan cigarettes, supplied by a friend who'd profited handsomely from the Bosnian war) and wiped sweat from his forehead. Apparently the evicted tenants hadn't gone quietly, berating him with legal threats and throwing cat food in his face.

'I thought there was a no-pets rule?' said Sheena, hilariously unconcerned for his wellbeing.

'Did they leave though?' I said. 'Are they out?'

He nodded gravely. 'They're gone.'

'Good,' said Sheena, filling her glass with an easy-drinking Crémant the owner had provided in exchange for our continued silence on the whereabouts of his wife. 'Did they question the deposit?'

'They said they're taking you to court.' he said, huffing his cig like a bagpipe.

'Oh well, nothing to worry about there then,' said Sheena. 'We're in the clear.'

Doorman looked at me nonplussed, unaware of our association with Wretchley.

'Leave that to us,' I said. 'Move in whenever you like.'

~

The tenants' solicitors served us with court papers (immediately thrown in the bin) and were demanding the return of their deposits plus damages and legal fees.

'They've got too much time on their hands,' said Sheena. 'Can't they just accept it and move on?'

'I know,' I said. 'If a landlord took our deposit I'd assume it was for a good reason.'

'Exactly,' she said. 'Maybe we need to start some kind of landlord protection society. Because right now we're being taken for mugs.'

Later we arrived at the Ten Hours club and found Lord Wretchley at the bar discussing the club's wine committee with the juror. His cheeks were ruddied and his gut protruded like an overstuffed compost bag.

'I don't know what to tell you, old sock. It's an abomination. Try it for yourself.'

The juror raised a wine glass to his lips and crumpled his face in disgust. 'My God, old man, you're right. That's bloody awful.'

Wretchley spotted us through the smoke and beckoned us over. 'Get over here, you two,' he said, his moustache bloodied with wine. 'Come and taste this, see what you think. Blasted wine committee's gone and chosen a blended grape variety. Can you believe it?'

I took a sip, and despite enjoying it immensely, wrinkled my nose and pretended to gag. 'Disgusting.' I said.

Sheena did the same, advising she needed five whiskies to wash the taste out of her mouth. 'Tastes like bin juice.' she said.

Wretchley patted us on the shoulders. 'Marvellous,' he said, smelling like a bonfire. 'Glad we're all on the same page. I'll assemble the committee and get this all straightened out. Bloody disaster, wouldn't you say?'

'Absolutely,' said Sheena. 'I can't believe it.'

Before he fussed off Sheena caught his arm. 'Could we talk to you about something?' she said, nervously picking a scab.

'Oh course, my dear,' he said, settling back into his stool. 'Has that bloody health secretary been trying to kidnap you? It's all the rage nowadays, you understand. Something about having power over vulnerables, I think.'

'No, no,' she said. 'Nothing like that.'

'Well if he does, try to break him down psychologically. When he feeds you, pretend you're his mother. Tell him it's okay to touch himself, that sort of thing. Hopefully you'll get away with a light thrashing.'

'Oh, okay,' she said, bemused. 'Thanks for the advice.' She paused and her eyes darted about the room.

'Anyway my dear,' he said. 'What did you want to talk to me about?'

'Yes, sorry,' she said, focusing. 'It's our tenants. They want to take us to court.'

Wretchley puffed his cheeks incredulously. 'I thought he's in a coma?' he said. 'Bloody thing's not woken up, has he?'

'No, it's not Ed,' she said. 'He's still unconscious, thank Christ. It's these blokes we evicted recently. They want their deposits back.'

'Oh God, I think I know the ones you mean,' he said. 'Those twits on the ground floor? Bloody pain in the knackers if you ask me.'

'Yes, them,' said Sheena. 'They sent us court papers.'

Lord Wretchley exhaled a handsome plume of smoke. 'Don't you worry, friends,' he said. 'You know the drill: call Hilary, get a court date, turn up, blah blah. Nothing to worry about.'

'This is becoming a bit of a habit with you two, eh?' said the juror. 'In and out of court like a pair of subprime mortgage lenders.'

'Ho ho,' chortled Wretchley. 'That was a funny old

time, eh? All that business with the financial crash. All those bankers running around like chickens? Bloody nuisance if you ask me.'

'You're right there, old man,' said the juror.

We left them laughing at foreclosed homes and shattered livelihoods and tore into a bottle of Warpecker.

'Best call Hilary Bell.' I said.

'Urgh, *court* again,' she grumbled. 'Another morning we won't be able to drink.'

I know, I said. *How awful.*

In truth I would've appreciated a morning off drinking. I'd been drunk or hungover every day for as long as I could remember, and the days on which I'd not been drunk I'd very much wished I had been.

Naturally we finished the bottle, hurling the empties at the bar boy's head like a coconut shy. He showed little resistance, glazed and numb to our torment. Wretchley later clarified that club members used him as a guinea pig on which to test the efficacy of drugs they'd smuggled back from business trips, rewarding him with handjobs once he'd weathered the adverse effects.

We later became entangled in a discussion about the minimum wage. Sheena and I thought it should be abolished and the money spent on specialist leisure facilities for the one percent, while the heath secretary thought that instead of money, low-skilled workers should be paid in goods like sheep's wool and teacakes. 'They'd love it,' he said. 'That's all they spend their wages on anyway.'

We nodded, conceding that he did, in fact, have a very good point.

'It's true,' said Sheena. 'That's all they buy. Probably the odd packet of crisps but mostly just teacakes.'

'Exactly!' said the health secretary. 'Maybe I'll mention it in Commons. Be good to see how the rest of the party feels.'

'You do that, old sock,' said Wretchley, tumbling up

beside us with a massive port and lemon. He seemed roaring drunk, more so than I'd ever seen him. 'Keep making those savings,' he slurred. 'More money for the Christmas party!'

We drank so much that we barely made it out of the club door the next morning, having to be hauled into the car by Doorman, saturated in sick. He drove us home and bundled us into the lift, dragging us into the living room and positioning a bottle of trafficker's rum on the table for when we woke up, knowing Sheena would erupt if she didn't have her morning drink.

Seven hours later I opened my eyes, winced in pain, gulped rum and tried desperately to go back to sleep.

It was evening when I woke fully. Sheena was in bed, screaming in pain, while the bottle of rum stood half-finished on the table. I joined in her chorus of screams, roaring until my throat dried out and constricted me to the point of breathlessness. Feeling no better whatsoever, I hauled myself onto the sofa and tried to catch my breath, panting like a Hollywood casting director.

'How can I feel this bad?' screamed Sheena from her bedroom. 'I only had one or two drinks!'

Baffling, I thought, trying to convince myself that I too had only had one or two drinks.

She tramped into the living room with a Thrushman's in her mouth and an inhaler in her hand. 'I've taken twenty-five paracetamol,' she said. 'And I still feel like death.'

In an effort to restore wellness, we opted for a lavish crab and tenderloin dinner, tipping the delivery boy in bottle tops we'd fished out of the bin.

'He'll probably be able to trade them with his pals,' said Sheena. 'Swap them for copper wire or something.'

'I suppose in a lot of ways it's better than giving him money.' I said.

'Yes,' she said. 'He'd have only spent it on remixes anyway.'

Bloated and defeated we retreated to bed after dinner, writing off the day and resolving to start afresh tomorrow. We had a lawyer to call.

CHAPTER 16

Hilary Bell's office was as immaculate as I remembered, his desk ornaments suggesting an extensive and formidable personal fortune. Sitting behind his desk with legs crossed like chopsticks, he fingered a fountain pen and flexed his jawbone. 'Another court date,' he said, his words brisk and snappy (presumably he was required to speak quickly to confuse slow-witted jurors). 'Tenants again?'

'Yes,' said Sheena. 'They want their deposits back.'

'And you're not willing to oblige?' he said.

'We've spent it.' I said, recalling the drooling steak dinner.

'Right.' he said.

'And they don't deserve it,' said Sheena. 'They *desecrated* our property. You should see the dirt. And the mould.'

'Have you mentioned this to our friend?'

'Yes,' I said. 'He's fine with it.'

'Good,' he said. 'As long as I know we'll win, I can prepare our defence accordingly.'

'We'll win,' she said. 'No doubt about it.'

Did Sheena's resolve ever falter? I didn't believe so. Every endeavour upon which she'd embarked had bore fruit, somehow netting us a total of five properties in an extraordinarily short timeframe. She was like a tractor pulling a chisel plow, blindly tearing up everything in her wake as she rumbled towards her next acquisition.

Hilary Bell extended his twig fingers and made some notes. We sat in silence, lulled by the scraping of the pen strokes.

'Can we smoke?' said Sheena, clicking her lighter irritably.

'Nope.' he said, not looking up. His tone was unambiguous: he wanted us to be quiet. We sat, suicidally bored, as he finished his notes and sipped thistle tea. I stared about the room, noting for the first time the personal effects positioned throughout. A pair of shoes sat beneath the coat stand: buffed black brogues, glossy as stag beetles; elegantly pocked with decorative perforations and hand-serrated toe caps. I'd little doubt they cost any less than the court costs for which we were currently liable.

'Good,' said Hilary Bell, briskly closing his folder. 'You should receive a court summons in the next few weeks. Same as before, don't get drunk beforehand, dress for the judge, keep quiet. Okay?'

'Yes.' we said, still quietly resentful of having to smarten up for a jury of commoners.

We exited Hilary Bell's office and headed straight for the Pig & Bucket, the manager of which was on sick leave due to his ongoing Lyme disease.

'I'm so bored of this,' said Sheena, scratching at the table with her house keys. 'Having to go to court every week just for trying to earn an honest living.'

'I know,' I said. 'Why won't they leave us alone? Landlords do this kind of thing all the time. Why are they picking on *us?*'

'Exactly,' she said. 'Although maybe it's just teething problems. A few bad tenants to begin with, then things will sort themselves out.'

I nodded hesitantly. 'I hope so.'

'What we really need,' she started, defiantly hosing us with spittle, 'is a change in the law.'

'What kind of a change?' I said, sure she was now on an

absolute hot streak of madness.

'Landlords need to claw back some rights,' she said. 'Get these tenants in line.'

'Like what?' I said. 'What kind of rights?'

'Like this whole deposit bullshit,' she said. 'Deposits should be ours to keep. To spend on whatever we like. A 'thank you' for letting them live in our property.'

'It *sounds* like a good idea,' I said. 'But how could we change the law? Where would we even start?'

'Start at the club,' she said. 'Ask the health secretary to pass a bill.'

'Would he do that?'

'Listen,' she said. 'How many of those club members are landlords?'

'All of them.' I said, quite honestly.

'Right. So they'd all benefit from this, wouldn't they?'

'Yes,' I said, 'I suppose they would.'

'So let's get down there,' she said. 'Let's go tomorrow.'

We drank till our brains were porridge, then phoned Doorman to come and collect us. He'd been at a union members' benefit gig, supporting the cause by distributing sausages to activists. He arrived in his knackered old shitheap and helped us inside like an overworked carer.

'Why don't you get a new car?' gurned Sheena. 'This one's a *piece of shit*.'

'My brother gave me this car,' he said, suddenly sombre. 'His dog died in it.'

'Oh how awful.' I blurted, checking my seat for canine skull fragments.

'He had to strangle it,' said Doorman. 'Poor thing kept biting his nutbag.'

'Good for him,' said Sheena. 'Dogs are pathetic anyway. And anyone who owns one is pathetic.'

I recalled Grandma's dog: a savage, drooling killer she doped with plant estrogen to exacerbate its aggression, resulting in childhood hospital visits and blood-sodden swaddling cloths. 'I hate dogs too.' I mumbled, barely comprehensible after the sousing I'd taken. 'They don't love you.'

Doorman quietened, driving joylessly while we stubbed cigs out on his seat fabric. Evidently he appreciated dogs despite their taking umbridge with his brother's ballsack. I strained to understand the attraction, especially after being told my sister's face would never be successfully pieced back together.

We tumbled upstairs to the apartment and chundered white slime into the kitchen sink. Had we eaten contaminated crabmeat?

~

With tiresome inevitability our court date arrived and once again we were forced out of our dressing gowns in order to convince the pleb chorus of our obvious innocence.

'Why don't they use legal experts on juries?' said Sheena, brushing her teeth for the first time in a month. 'How can they trust the general public to reach an educated verdict?'

'I don't understand it either,' I said. 'Surely the public's busy with other things like cake shows and musicals? They can't possibly be expected to make such important decisions.'

'Thank God for Wretchley,' she said, slathering her armpits in lavender block. 'I don't know what we'd do if we didn't have him.'

'We'd probably be rotting in prison,' I said. 'Fighting gang members for soap rations.'

'Sounds like a party,' she said, blobbing cosmetic paste over her facial sores. 'Sign me up.'

It was dark and drizzling and Doorman was waiting outside, his trusted banger spluttering like a hospice patient. 'Morning.' he said, opening the door for us. (He was still reassuringly servile.)

'God, I need a drink,' said Sheena. 'Can we stop at a

pub first?'

Doorman held a newspaper over her head, honourably shielding her hair from the rain. 'Nowhere's open I'm afraid, Madam,' he said. 'Too early.'

'Pissing licensing laws,' muttered Sheena. 'Let's talk to the health secretary about those as well. Make some changes.'

'Good idea,' I said. 'Who even makes these laws?'

'God knows,' she said. 'But whoever it is deserves to hang.'

We were met at the courthouse by a surging assembly of photographers and newspeople, all coated in sopping rain macs that lent them the look of an encroaching cultist flock.

'Why are there so many of them?' said Sheena. 'There's twice as many as last time.'

'I don't know.' I said, flummoxed. Surely this was a straightforward domestic squabble with little interest to the public?

Doorman drove up to the curb and eased gingerly through the crush. He was cautious despite our demands for him to flatten them. 'They're people too.' he said, a naive idiom we met with derisory snorts.

'*People?*' sneered Sheena. 'Do me a favour.'

We barged the car doors open and fortuitously knocked a couple of photographers to the ground, prompting a wry comment from Sheena about the gutter press. Microphones were thrust at us as we jostled through the scrum, kicking and thrashing at journalists like they were swarming bats.

'Are you the new Peter Rachman?' one journalist cawed.

'Are you leading the new wave of slum landlords?' barked another.

My head was swivelling. 'What?' I said. 'I don't -'

'Do you endorse rent slavery?'

'Are you at the forefront of a new generation of

housing poverty?'

Hilary Bell appeared out of the throng and shunted us inside. We emerged in the entrance hall, dripping and dazed.

'What was *that?*' spat Sheena.

'Press,' said Hilary Bell briskly. 'They think something's up.'

'But we've done nothing wrong,' she said. 'We just took back what was ours.'

'That might well be the case,' he said. 'But there's a housing crisis at the moment. The rental market's being scrutinised. And you two seem to be getting yourselves a reputation.'

'What do you mean?' I said. 'Are we famous?'

He deliberated. 'Let's see how today goes. We'll reassess after the fact.'

We muddled into the courtroom, no longer strangers to the process, and sat in silence. Lord Wretchley appeared, robed and fabulous, and invited the newspeople to curb their gabbing. As before, Hilary Bell made his opening statement, charming the jury like a child-grooming priest. The prosecution, predictably, was ineffectual: inert mumblings about slum landlords and abuses of power that we'd have scoffed at had Hilary Bell not oathed us into silence.

Wretchley didn't even bother calling witnesses, bustling through the proceedings without care or compassion. The two tenants that were suing us, stubbly and comfortably fed, visibly fizzed with anger at the slapdash approach being taken. They whispered to their lawyer, hissing and urgent like diamond pythons. Noticing this, Wretchley calmly reprimanded them, subtextually implying their discontent was unacceptable and had just lost them the case.

It concluded quickly, with the jury delivering a Not Guilty verdict as expected. Wretchley gavelled out the session and we left the courtroom, smug and nonchalant.

'You two are criminals!' shrieked one of the tenants, kicking up a scene in the corridor outside.

'Don't say a word.' urged Hilary Bell.

'Drop dead, scum!' screamed back Sheena, ignoring his spineless warnings.

'You should be locked up!' he bawled, clearly deranged. Who would lock *us* up?

'You should be killed!' roared Sheena.

Hilary Bell tried to hush her like a mortified parent.

'We've done nothing wrong!' she crowed. 'You destroyed our property!'

The tenant was ushered away, back to debtor's prison or wherever the hell he belonged.

Hilary Bell frogmarched us down a deserted corridor, glowering as if he'd just seen a play. 'You two, this way.' he said, sounding eerily like Aunt Sandra before she'd drowned her health visitors.

'You can't *do* that,' he hissed. 'Not with all these reporters around.'

'But did you hear what he said?' said Sheena. 'He's a tosser!'

'That may be true,' he said. 'But that *tosser's* probably outside right now, telling the newspapers that you threatened to kill him.'

'He can tell them whatever he likes,' she said. 'They're not going to print it.'

~

Contrary to Sheena's thoughts on the matter, the press were delighted by the tenant's claims, granting us some (though not much) newspaper coverage. It was mostly buried in the latter pages and petered out over a matter of days.

'Why aren't we front page news?' she said, her mouth filled with Pule, a Serbian donkey cheese that cost more than Mum's deathmask.

'I don't know,' I said. 'Surely we're more important than whatever the hell they're reporting on today?'

The front page in question featured a libellous puff piece about a refugee who'd supposedly been awarded a nine-bedroom city mansion by a local left-wing councillor hellbent on transforming British high streets into multinational prison ghettos.

'Is any of this true?' I said, scanning down the article. 'Was he really given two million pounds' worth of lawn ornaments?'

'There must be *some* truth in it,' she said. 'Otherwise they wouldn't print it.'

I remained dubious. One paragraph explained how the refugee had been visited by left-wing terror groups who camped on his roof, burned the St. George's cross and danced to Stalinist rave music.

'We're on page twenty-two,' said Sheena. 'Page *twenty-two*. It's a kick in the teeth. Especially since we made such an effort to dress up, not drink, blah blah blah. Why did those photographers even bother turning up?'

'I don't know,' I said. 'Maybe it was a slow news day. That's what Hilary Bell said.'

'Maybe.' she said. She spooned tobacco into her mouth and pulled on a snakeskin gilet. 'Anyway, it doesn't matter now. Let's get to the club. We need to see the health secretary.'

Doorman drove us to the Ten Hours and gave us an update on the flats he now guarded. 'The old woman's no problem,' he said, crunching on a pig biscuit. 'She'll be dead soon.'

'Good,' said Sheena. 'Have a root around her flat when she carks it. See if there's anything worth taking.'

'You can get fifty pounds for a good zimmer frame these days,' I said. 'Especially if it's got a mounted carry basket.'

'Exactly,' said Sheena. 'Any old junk like that, get it sold. She's probably got a heap of antiques up there as well. Porcelain cats and so on.'

'What about the girls?' I said. 'The *students?* I pealed off the word with a notable disgust, impatient for them to finish their degrees and end up in demoralising office jobs with no relevance whatsoever to their areas of study.

'They're crazy,' he said. 'I don't know how they do it every night.'

'Do what?' I said.

'Everything,' he said. 'Drink, drugs, gangbangs, the lot.'

I shuddered at the mention of students, recalling their sick games and depraved torments from my previous life.

'But their rent comes in every month,' said Sheena. 'So we couldn't care less what they do.'

'I suppose not.' I said, trying to judge them purely as revenue streams.

'Is there anything else?' I said. 'Anything wrong with the building?'

'Oh everything,' he said. 'Cracked windows, leaking light fittings, nothing works. It's horrendous.'

'Fine,' said Sheena. 'Sounds like normal wear and tear to me.'

He dropped us outside the club and we fumbled inside, chattering with cold. Despite being autumn it was already debilitatingly icy and our breath uncurled from our mouths like ghostly blue farts.

'Sounds like everything's going well at the flats.' I said, unsure whether I knew the difference between fantasy and reality anymore.

'Oh yes,' she said. 'It's like we're running a five-star hotel.'

The bar room was dark and I heard distant sex noises. Were they bonking each other? The health secretary was slouched at the bar, flicking lit matches at the bar boy and sucking lines of cocaine off a government white paper on dementia care.

'Hi,' said Sheena. 'Could we talk to you? It's very important.'

'Of course, little bird,' he said. 'Would you like a drink? I'm told the wine's still in negotiation but the whisky's really hitting the spot.'

'Yes that'd be great,' she said. 'Can we have the bottle?'

'Oh, but of course!' he said. 'Good strategy. Means you don't have to keep asking *him* for top ups.' He motioned to the bar boy. 'Little devil.' He poured us three Warpeckers each and nudged the cocaine in our direction. 'Help yourselves,' he said. 'I'll expense it all back.'

We blasted ourselves full of drink and drugs before settling down to business.

'Basically, we think landlords get a bad deal.' said Sheena, rubbing her gums with a shuddering finger.

'Yes, we get a really bad deal.' I said, spiritedly. I felt *wonderful.* 'We need more rights.'

'More rights for us,' said Sheena. 'That's it. That's what we want. More rights.'

'Right,' said the health secretary. 'More rights. That sounds like a great idea. Landlords deserve to be respected, don't you think? These bloody tenants think they can walk all over us. That's not right.'

'Right!' cried Sheena. 'Respect. That's what we want. More respect. Tenants think they can do anything they like. They don't respect us.'

'You're right!' said the health secretary, hurling back another drink and throwing the glass at the bar boy. 'We need to have a look at these tenants' rights. See what we can change.'

'Can you do that?' I said. 'Can you do that now?'

'I'll put a bill together and raise it in commons,' he said. 'I can't imagine anyone will oppose it. We're all bloody landlords!'

'Amazing, amazing,' said Sheena. 'What kind of things shall we put in it?'

'Whatever you like,' he said. 'What would you like?'

'This nonsense about paying for repairs,' she said, her eye twitching spasmodically. 'It's crazy. If a tenant breaks something they should pay to get it fixed.'

'I agree, I agree,' I said. 'Do they think we're all millionaires?'

'Right, great. That'll be our first point.' He scrawled notes, frantically, on the white paper, adding diagrams of hanging stickmen. We drew up the majority of the bill right there, laughing deliriously as we eroded the rights of tenants for the next four years. (It'd take a complete change in government to overturn what we did that night.) According to our bill, there'd be no requirement for landlords to give twenty-four hours' notice before entering the property, and they could even commandeer tenants' beds should they require them. Also scrapped was the deposit protection scheme, the idea that a tenant's deposit would be held securely by an impartial third party who'd pay out once an agreement had been reached.

'That's ridiculous,' said Sheena. 'The deposit should go straight to the landlord and should only be refundable in exceptional circumstances. Otherwise we keep it without question.'

'Great idea, great idea.' said the health secretary, now staggeringly drunk. We finalised the details and he promised he'd raise it the first chance he got. 'No point waiting around,' he said. 'Let's get it done!'

We toasted our good work and finished the bottle of Warpecker. It was then that Lord Wretchley appeared, flushed and uncharacteristically demure. He was breathing heavily and affixing plasters to his hand.

'What happened to you, old man?' bawled the health secretary, slapping him like a choking infant.

Wretchley glowered at him and dabbed blood from his hand with a handkerchief.

'Are they - bite marks?' said Sheena, noting his injury.

He huffed and exhaled a cloud of smoke. 'No no,' he said, regaining his composure. 'Nothing like that, my dear.' He covered the wound with plaster and quickly inflated back to health. 'What's going on here then, old sock?' he said, gesturing to the scribbled notes. 'Planning something splendid?'

The health secretary outlined the new bill and Wretchley threw his head back like a Pez dispenser. 'Sounds like a smashing idea,' he said. 'Landlords get a bloody raw deal sometimes. Glad you're giving things a good shake-up.'

The health secretary generously doled out cocaine, chopping out increasingly plump and punishing lines as he grew irreparably ravaged. He eventually collapsed in a toilet having used the white paper to smear excrement across the cubicle walls.

Meanwhile we sat, sozzled, with our heads on the bar, eyes like kidney beans and throats as dry as textbooks.

'What're your plans for the rest of the evening?' said Lord Wretchley, cradling a port and lemon. 'It's Saturday, you know. Why don't you go and find a party? Have a bit of fun. You've been working awfully hard with this tiresome bill business.'

'You're right,' said Sheena. 'We *have* been working hard. We deserve to have some fun.'

'But -' I started. 'Why don't we just stay here?'

'Obviously you're always welcome here, old chap,' he said. 'But we all need some fresh stimuli every now and again, don't you think?'

'Problem is we don't know anyone having a party.' I said.

'Oh I'm sure you do,' he said. 'What about those student girls of yours?'

'You mean our tenants?' said Sheena.

'Yes,' he purred. 'Why don't you go and meet them? Have a drink? Get to know each other? Very important to meet your tenants you know. Keeps them sweet and malleable.'

Was he asking us or telling us? 'Is that a good idea?' I said. 'Should we be mingling with tenants?'

'Maybe you're right,' he said. 'Might be a bit much. You

don't want to go in there mob-handed. Why don't you stay here and you -' he gestured to Sheena. 'You go and meet them first. Might be easier.'

This seemed like a reasonable suggestion given my unswerving hatred of students.

'Okay, maybe -' said Sheena.

'Smashing!' he said. 'That's settled then. You go and meet the little rotters, we'll stay here and make sure that bloody health secretary's alright.'

'Oh, okay -' said Sheena, somewhat bemused.

'I'll fetch you a car.' he said, disappearing behind the bar.

'Are you sure you want to go?' I said. 'They are *students* after all. They might make you defecate into a disco ball.'

'It'll be fine,' she said. 'I've not been to a student party for years. It'll be good to relive it all.'

Wretchley reappeared and waved towards the door. 'Your transport.' he said, ferociously charming. Flapping goodbye, Sheena skittered off, jittering like a loose bundle of twigs.

'She'll have a whale of a time,' he said. 'I've no doubt these students get up to all sorts nowadays. In my day it was all rowing clubs and masturbation rituals. How times must've changed!'

Once Sheena was gone, Wretchley loosened like a slackened anus and made rambunctious remarks about The Cat Being Away. I immediately felt strangely vulnerable and wanted very much to leave. 'I might head home,' I said. 'I think I left the oven on.'

'Nasty business that, old sock,' said Wretchley. 'Happened to a local cafe owner recently. His poor wife suffered terribly.'

'How awful,' I said, not remotely stirred. 'But I really must go.'

He waved me off and disappeared into the crowd, slapping mens' backs and gobbling his cigar. I wondered if Sheena was enjoying the party, immensely thrilled not to be there myself. Doorman was sleeping like a nightwatchman as I yanked open his car door and fell inside, breathless with cold.

'Just you tonight?' he said.

'Sheena's gone to a party,' I said. 'With *students*.' I sounded as disgusted as if I were watching a musical.

'Free education for all.' he said, unhelpfully.

I sulked all the way home.

CHAPTER 17

I awoke with scant suspicion of what'd occurred during the night. The apartment was empty and I assumed Sheena had stayed out all night taking speed and gangbanging with the students. (When I'd lived with students they'd sleep all day and arise like ghouls at bedtime, at which point they'd pelt glass bottles at my door and scream parricidal threats at the top of their lungs.)

It was a vile prospect but not one I begrudged her: her university days had been so monstrously horrible she was firmly deserving of a second chance. It also granted me a temporary spell of solitude, something I'd stridently avoided since the unparalleled misery of my renting days, a woeful nadir during which I'd lie alone in a freezing bedsit with only powdered egg for sustenance.

Day shrivelled into night and still Sheena hadn't returned. I drank eight cans of *Murgs*, a Latvian chemical lager, and dozed off, dreaming of students pulling my toenails out. It was a sweaty, fitful sleep and I awoke several times gasping for alcohol. I arose at midday unrested and sick, my mouth as dry as a terrestrial drama series. I shuffled to the kitchen and gargled salt water which I retched back into the sink, my nostrils flared and streaming. With shuddering hands I poured Sheena's breakfast whisky and swayed towards her bedroom. I rapped on the door and expected the usual scream as she awoke, shelled by ceaseless bolts of pain. No reply. I knocked again. 'Sheena?' I said. 'Are you awake?'

No reply. Had she succumbed to her excesses and died at last? Her funeral would no doubt be a sparsely-attended washout: a brisk ceremony in a Welsh chapel conducted by a vicar preoccupied with community ping-pong scores. I left the whisky on the countertop and climbed onto the sofa, enswathing myself in its pillowy warmth.

Several hours later I woke again, this time from a second, more restorative, sleep. The glass sat untouched where I'd left it. Could she really have died?

Feeling marginally more invigorated, I approached her door and eased open the handle. 'Sheena?' I said, my head still pulsing with beer shock. 'Are you asleep?'

I snapped on the light. She wasn't here. The bed was fussy and unmade and brandy miniatures cluttered the table like shotgun shells. Very suddenly I panicked, wondering how I'd manage the finances were she to have carked it. Could I just bury our money in a bone cave?

I checked under the bed (often she'd fall out of bed, drunk, and wake up with a mouthful of shagpile) but found nothing. I checked the wardrobe but, as expected, it contained only lambswool and a decomissioned nebuliser.

There was little else to check. It was much like an upmarket hotel room - brushed steel fixtures, leather-backed reading chair - that she'd personalised by tacking property listings to the walls.

I checked the bathroom, the lav, the balcony, with no luck. Was she still at the students' party?

Despite my concern I reasoned she was a steadfast, autonomous adult who could do whatever the hell she liked, and had probably embarked on a well-earned weekend bender. And why not? We'd both worked so hard recently, weathering tenants and court dates, that we deserved to indulge a little. Perhaps I could overcome my reservations and join the party?

Predictably, Sheena's phone was dead, so I phoned Doorman; a pre-emptive measure to ensure the party was still, in fact, in full swing.

'Sheena?' he said, sounding puzzled. 'I've not seen her. Isn't she with you?'

'No,' I said. 'She's at the flats. She's at a party with the students on the first floor.'

He paused. 'I was up there earlier,' he said. 'Fixing their ballcock. They said they'd never even met you.'

I didn't say a word. Was I in a film?

'They said they wanted to meet you because they heard you both liked getting shitfaced.'

'But -' I said, uncomprehending. 'That's where she went. I don't understand. Were they joking? Were they drunk?'

'Of *course* they were drunk,' he said. 'They're students. But they weren't joking. They didn't even know your names.'

'So where's Sheena?' I said, naively expecting him to care.

'I don't know,' he said. 'But I really have to go. I'm photographing a dyspeptic folk singer tonight.'

Was he lying to me? 'I need you to come and get me,' I said. 'I need to speak to the students.'

The phone blinked, unhearing. He'd gone.

Furiously, I hurled it at the wall. Could I evict him as punishment for his insubordination?

I needed to see the students and confirm their story. I assumed they were mistaken, drunkenly identifying Sheena as one of their own and ignoring her as the party rolled towards oblivion. I'd probably arrive and find her unconscious in a laundry hamper, I thought. But how might I get there? We'd been blacklisted by the local cab firms (they who considered themselves fit only for royalty) and Doorman was busy trying to stave off thoughts of suicide. Short of hiring a limousine - an impossibility given our current cashflow problems - I had only one option. I'd need to travel by bus. *Bus*. How far I'd fallen. Like a scrabbling rat in a shipping container.

The bus service was currently in the midst of a dispute between the operator and the drivers' union, a clash seemingly without resolution. The operator, a European war conglomerate with interests in militarised bot armies and freelance sleeper cells, was determined to restrict the drivers' beer allowance to a paltry three pints per shift. Such a stipulation was deemed unworkable by the union, who demanded adherence to the previous eight-pint stricture, a measure that claimed only two hundred lives a year on the roads. The death toll would surely rise, they claimed, if drivers were grumpy and felt their rights were being trampled.

Such conflict ensured the buses ran intermittently at best, often rolling up hours after the scheduled arrival time and heaving with tetchy office workers, sallow and pocked with sweat, bemoaning the fact they'd ever been born.

Steeling myself in a sturdy microfleece, I walked a mile to the nearest bus stop. It was a tiny plastic lean-to through which the wind whooshed like an industrial steam jet. I leaned on the plastic half-bench (not quite wide enough to sit on) and wondered how I might possibly have been cursed with such rotten luck. Yesterday I had a *chauffeur* for heaven's sake. What crimes must I have committed in a previous life that I might be condemned to such torment? An hour later a bus wheezed along, heavy with faceless human scum. They were squeezed against the windows with their faces moist and ruddied like murderous widowers. Would they even let me on?

The door opened and I wedged myself in, thumping past commuters in the hope I'd injure at least one or two of them. The bus rumbled off but we stopped again after five minutes for the driver to enjoy a gentle afternoon pint.

An hour later I alighted at Plugwood Lock. My mouth was sticky and my temper was shredded, having been jostled senseless by coated bodies and oversized backpacks. (Were the commuters going *camping?*) I'd quaffed three tins of *Murgs* on the bus but needed an ocean more if I were to restabilize. Once reunited with Sheena I'd suggest we visit the Pig & Bucket and drink ourselves blind in an effort to calm my jangled nerves.

I approached the flats and picked my way through the front garden. It was littered with false teeth and perished jockstraps and I noticed the corpse of a mutilated cat on the doorstep. Probably a student blood ritual, I thought.

I entered the building and immediately began wheezing and huffing as the mould spores entered my respiratory system. I let myself into Doorman's flat (my flat, really) for a cursory snoop and recoiled immediately. It smelt like a stagnant canal. I picked a jumper from a nearby pile of clothes and held it over my nose but it, too, smelt stale and mouldy. Didn't he have a washing machine? I crept through to the kitchen and confirmed that no, he didn't have a washing machine, instead there sat a basin half-filled with black water and rags.

All seems fine here, I thought, as deluded as a dog lover. *He probably doesn't even need a washing machine.*

I returned to the hall and ascended the stairs. They creaked like pensioners' joints and I feared they might collapse like Grandpa's mental health.

The first floor was, impossibly, even more decimated than the ground. Broken bottles littered the hallway and the floor was carpeted with cig butts, condoms, speed wraps, tobacco strands. I picked my way through the wreckage and approached the students' door. Poor Sheena, I thought. She's probably inside right now, unconscious on a vomit-caked mattress or worse, being made to listen to somebody play an acoustic guitar. I knocked on the door. No answer. I knocked again, this time hammering like a bailiff. No reply. Sick of knocking, I let myself in because, in fairness, it was my flat.

Inside was a terrifying shitheap. The carpet was studded with cig burns and the walls were stained a sallow brown.

The floorplan matched Doorman's so I clattered through a pile of beer cans to the safety of the kitchen. At the kitchen table was a student, slumped unconscious and hopefully dead.

'Hey student,' I said. 'Where's Sheena?'

She groaned softly.

'Is she here?' I said. 'Is Sheena here?'

The student, a rat-tailed girl in a Barbour jacket, lifted her head and stared at me. Her eyes were black and she had fag ash around her mouth. Was she a zombie? 'Hey, who are you?' she said.

'I'm your landlord,' I said. 'I'm looking for Sheena. Where is she?'

'Who's Sheena?' she said, immediately lighting a cig. 'And aren't you supposed to give notice before you come round?'

'No, no,' I said assuredly. 'The law's changing. Landlords can come round whenever they like.'

'That's bullshit.' she said.

'Look, student,' I said. 'I'm not here for sexual favours or whatever the hell landlords normally come round for. I just need to find Sheena. She's not been home for days. Where is she?'

'Seriously, who's Sheena?' said the student, clearly stoned or deranged. 'Is she your wife or something?'

'Oh no,' I said. 'We've never shared an attraction. We live together. We're landlords.'

'Hang about -' her eyes widened as if meeting a celebrity. 'Are you the slum landlord I saw on the news?'

'What do you mean?' I said. 'Everything we do is perfectly legal and ethical.'

'You *are*,' she said, stubbing her cig out on a nearby plate. 'I recognise your face.'

I tensed, mentally resolving to evict her at the earliest opportunity.

'You were in court for evicting those lads downstairs and stealing their deposits. Yes! That makes sense.'

'Look student,' I said. 'I don't know what you're talking about. We own this building and we've not done a single thing wrong. They only wrote about us because it was a slow news day.'

She lit another cig and offered me one. *Don't mind if I do, thanks,* I thought, huffing in a hearty lungful. I took a seat at the table and sensed the atmosphere thawing somehow. 'So anyway,' I said, now markedly less antsy. 'She was here two nights ago for a party. A car dropped her off.'

I showed her a photograph of Sheena: it'd been taken seconds before she'd emptied a pint of lager over a football fan's head and her eyes glowed with bloodlust. (The incident had earned her a round of applause from the assembled pubgoers, many of whom joined her in dousing the halfwit in phlegm and drinks.)

'Honestly, I don't know what you're talking about,' she said. 'I've never seen her before in my life.' She clicked on the kettle. 'Did she come in a cab? Have you phoned the cab company?'

I hesitated. 'Erm, no -' I said.

'So, what?' she said. 'Did she drive here?'

'No,' I said. 'Somebody dropped her off.'

'Okay, so who dropped her off? Have you spoken to them?'

'No -' I said again, perfectly aware of how useless I now sounded.

The kettle began rumbling.

'Shouldn't you do that first?' she said.

'Er, okay, yes -' I said dumbly. How had I been outsmarted by a *student*?

'But she's definitely not been here,' she said. 'We had a quiet weekend. Only about thirty or forty people. I would've noticed a new face.'

I finished the cig and rose. 'Thanks then, student,' I said, surprised to feel a warmth rising inside me. The kettle thundered to its climax.

'We'll give you a call if she comes by,' she said. 'I hope you find her.'

I tramped out, wished the student well (had I gone mad?) and found myself back in the hallway. I surveyed the second flight of stairs and deliberated checking on the old woman. *She's probably fine*, I thought, envisaging opulent lodgings filled with antique clocks and extravagant sherries. *It must be like a palace up there*, I thought.

I strode back to the bus stop, determined to get to the Ten Hours club. Lord Wretchley would surely know who'd driven Sheena that night. I dearly hoped nothing bad had happened to her: I was terrible with equity forms and banking documentation. And would I be expected to make the funeral arrangements if she'd been killed? Supposedly such events cost thousands; you couldn't simply toss the body off a roof and hope it was eaten by foxes. I could always sell one of the flats, I reasoned, untroubled by the thought of turfing out Doorman and trousering a cool million for the property.

I waited at the bus stop for two hours before a bus appeared. The driver was chugging from a beer bottle and waved me on without payment. 'We won!' he said, grinning fatuously. 'Up the workers!'

Doorman would be thrilled. The operator had acquiesced to the union's demands and relented on the issue of beer drinking at work. *Good for them*, I thought, hoping such humanity might soon extend to other fields of employment like aviation and medicine.

The driver rattled and shunted towards town, hitting cyclists with the breezy recklessness of religious pressure groups. I exited at the bus stop nearest the club and scrambled down the iron steps. Being late afternoon, the place was quiet, with only a clutch of MPs drinking port and vacuuming up cocaine.

The bar boy was at his post, sucking a cig and holding his hands out in front of him. They were shaking - no doubt a result of the test medicines he'd been administered

- but he seemed incapable of reacting with anything besides numb stupefaction. Did he even know where he was?

'Hey,' I said, throwing an olive at his head. 'Where's Lord Wretchley? Is he here?'

He gazed at me and his mouth opened very slowly. He looked like he wanted to say something but produced no sound.

'What are you trying to say?' I said, irritated at his vegetative state. 'Is Wretchley here?'

He set a glass in front of me and filled it with Warpecker, his shuddering hands spilling dribbles and droplets all over the bar.

'Thanks -' I said, vaguely concerned for his wellbeing. He was *grey*. 'Are you okay?' I said, so earnest I deserved a Samaritan's commendation. He moved his head up and down very slowly, opening and closing his mouth like a flatfish. I assumed he was fine and scanned the room for Wretchley. He wasn't here. I noticed the health secretary at a corner table. He was unwell and was using banknotes to blow his nose.

'Hi,' I said. 'Are you okay?'

'Urgh, hello old chap,' he said. 'I've come down with this bloody flu that's doing the rounds. Nasty business.'

'Have you had a Lemsip?' I said.

'I've tried everything old boy. Coke, prozzies, the lot. Can't shift it.'

I wanted to say *why don't you try soup and an early night* but something told me that simply wasn't an option.

'Have you seen Lord Wretchley?' I said. 'I need to find him.'

He shifted with a palpable unease. 'Oh no, old chap,' he said. 'I've not seen him for days. He's been ever so busy. Court cases and so forth.'

Why did he sound like he was lying to me? 'Do you know if he'll be here tonight?'

'Couldn't say, old boy,' he said. 'I've been out of the

loop for a while. Been in bed with this bloody flu.'

'If you see him could you tell him I'm looking for him?'

'Of course, old thing,' he said, hoofing another nostrilful of coke. 'I'll make it my top priority.' (I'd heard him say exactly the same thing when promising not to make nurses clean hospital toilets for no extra pay, an assurance that'd slipped down the agenda immediately following the last election.)

I sat at the bar and tried to clear my head by drinking ten whiskies. Where on earth could she be?

'Hello old chap,' came a voice. 'You look dreadful! What on earth's the matter?'

It was the juror who'd sold us the flats. He was swaying drunk and clutching a newspaper.

'I'm looking for Sheena,' I said. She's not been home for days and I can't get in touch with her. Do you know where she is?'

'What rotten luck, old thing. Still, we all lose things from time to time. I lost my favourite nutcracker last week. Terrible business. Sacked my cleaner over it.'

How awful, I slurred.

'So how are those flats working out for you?' he said, snaking his arm around me. 'Great little investment, eh? Needs a lick of paint but that's easily sorted. Chap I knew added his DIY costs to his tenants' rent. Let the little bastards pay for it themselves, don't you agree? You should add that to this bill you're pushing through parliament. It'd save us landlords a hell of a lot of money.'

'Okay,' I said. 'I'll mention it to the health secretary.'

He eyed me with fraternal sympathy. 'You seem sad old chap. Why don't we go and have some fun? Take your mind off this nasty kidnapping business.'

I suddenly focused. 'What?' I said. 'What kidnapping business? Who's been kidnapped?'

'Oh I just meant -' he shifted uneasily. 'All these kidnappings. You're probably thinking something like that's happened to poor Sheena.'

In fact, such a thought hadn't crossed my mind. I hoped she'd been on a prolonged bender and would reappear once the drugs had worn off.

'Sorry old chap, got to run,' he said, unsubtly edging away from me. 'Heaps to do you understand. Court cases and so on.'

Why were they all acting so peculiarly? I leaned back against the bar and quaffed another Warpecker. I felt like a travelling salesman after settling his brothel bill: drunk, worthless and alone. I nodded at the bar boy for another drink and he slid it towards me. Unusually he'd set the glass atop a napkin. Had I been spilling? I lifted the tumbler and took a punishing chug, focusing vaguely on the napkin. On it were written five words that immediately caused my mouth to fall open and whisky to dribble down my chin: *I KNOW WHERE SHE IS.*

I stared at the bar boy, then back at the napkin. The words had been scrawled like cobwebs, penmanship I attributed to the neutering effects of the drugs. He stared at me with empty, diaphanous eyes. His hands were shaking. I looked about me. There was nobody in earshot. 'Where?' I hissed. 'Where is she?'

He nodded into the bar room. I turned around. 'What, she's here?' I said.

He nodded again, only slightly more purposefully. It seemed he was trying to point someone out to me. I followed his gaze. It rested on a corner table: the table at which the health secretary was folding banknotes into origami swastikas.

'Him?' I said. 'He's got her?'

The bar boy nodded again. I hissed more questions but he'd become distracted by a spiralling bluebottle.

'Is she okay?' I said. 'Where's he taken her?'

He didn't answer, instead taking my glass and turning his back to me. He turned back and thrust me another drink. I noticed there were several patrons further down the bar, laughing as they defaced pictures of refugees in the newspaper. I lifted the glass and squinted at the napkin he'd slipped underneath. Scratched onto it was an address: *48 POGGLE STREET CRUMBFORD*. Nothing more. Without a word he edged away and served the other customers.

I trousered the napkins and pretended nothing had happened. Why was the bar boy helping me? Evidently he held a grudge against the health secretary but had little to gain by assisting Sheena and I. If anything, he'd be persecuted more were they to learn of his careless snitching. Perhaps he simply disapproved of kidnapping, I thought, recalling a time in my life when I'd *loved* to have been kidnapped; the thought of a rent-free shed or basement exciting me immeasurably.

Eager not to arouse suspicion, but also quite contentedly drunk, I sat at the bar and drank myself sick for a few more hours, chaining Thrushman's like a teenaged babysitter. I decided not to go home, instead I'd take the bus to Doorman's flat (my flat, really), and request he assist with Sheena's extraction the following day. I tottered towards the door and waved goodbye to the various dignitaries, unaware it'd be the last time I'd ever set foot inside the Ten Hours club.

The street outside was freezing and rain gushed down like urinary ejaculate. I ran to the bus stop and only had to wait half an hour before a bus rolled up. I assumed the improved service was the result of the resolved dispute between the drivers and their besuited overlords.

Puréed across the front of the bus were the remains of a cyclist, evidently killed due to reckless hand signalling. I boarded and the driver waived my fare, merrily gulping from a jumbo beer bottle and humming to ambient techno.

'Let it ride, bro,' he said, affecting a strange, transatlantic drawl.

I took a seat near the back and glared at the pouring sleet outside. My clothes were saturated and I sneezed repeatedly, spattering the windowpane with mucus before wiping my nose on the seat upholstery.

The night was so black it felt like we were shuttling through space. I squinted to make out the shapes of cars and fences, reassuring myself that we weren't in fact *en route* to Saturn.

I alighted at Plugwood Lock and noticed the bus driver had cracked open a second beer. *You deserve it*, I thought, imagining how dreadful it must be ferrying commuters around all day. My commuting days, thankfully now fading from memory, were a clammy, treacly nightmare brightened only by the distant hope that someone, somewhere, might throw themselves in front of a train.

I let myself into the building and sputtered through the hallway. There was post scattered across the floor and puddles of black water rippling with pondlife. *Why don't they clean this mess up?* I thought, irritated the tenants were so disrespecting of my precious investment. Once Sheena was back in the fold we'd enact a far more brutal cleaning regime, adding any supplementary cleaning costs (scouring pads, degreaser) to their rent. How dare they treat our portfolio with anything less than unquestioning reverence?

I knocked on Doorman's door and he appeared, pudgy and bedraggled, to greet me.

'Can I help, sir?' he said, still reassuringly deferent.

'I need your car,' I said, barrelling inside. 'We need to find Sheena.'

'Where is she?' he said, clicking on the kettle.

'Here, look,' I said, thrusting the napkin at him. 'She's been kidnapped by the health secretary.'

'My God,' he said. 'Is she alright?'

'I don't know, Doorman,' I said. 'I hope so.'

His flat was as vile as I'd remembered. With the light on I was able to see, in greater detail, the spare and sorrowful decor he was required to live with (out of spite, we'd forbidden him from personalising it in any way whatsoever). The walls were popcorned and painted a dirty lilac, while above the fireplace were affixed a terrifying set of red antlers that suggested an imminent human sacrifice. On a corner table stood a lamp whose lampshade resembled seaweed and which soaked the room in a dirty grey light.

'Looks lovely in here.' I said, calmly lying through my teeth.

'Redistribution of property.' he said, weakly affirming his convictions.

'Anyway,' I said, shutting him up immediately. 'We need to get to Poggle Street. Do you know where that is?'

He had a street map pinned to the wall (we'd later penalise him for the tack marks) and traced a line with his finger. 'It's in Crumbford.' he said.

'Yes I know it's in Crumbford,' I said. 'Can you drive us there?'

'It's a long way out,' he said. 'It's quite remote.'

Thanks for the ordnance survey briefing, I thought.

'I suppose I can drive there, yes.' he said.

'Great,' I said. 'We'll go tomorrow evening, when it's dark. Right now I need to use your bed. I'm very tired.'

He stared about the room, clearly unhappy with my request. 'I'm not sure about that, sir.'

'It's the law,' I said, almost telling the truth.

'What about the sofa?' he said. 'Maybe you could sleep there? It's comfortable.'

The sofa was a shabby, faux-leather monstrosity that looked very much like a pile of binbags. Within its plasticky creases was crusty food residue and I wondered how many strains of virus it was incubating. 'No, you have the sofa,' I said. 'I need the bed. It's the law.'

'Well, I suppose so, if it's the law,' he said, despondent and trampled. 'Bedroom's this way.'

He led me through the kitchen and squeezed open a side door. Inside the walls were papered with posters for various demonstrations and rallies, none of which I assumed had made a scrap of difference to government policy.

'I try to do my bit.' he said, by way of explanation.

I pitied his deluded stupidity: he could attend a million protest marches and still not make one shred of difference. The only way to affect change was to become drinking buddies with politicians and high court judges, something from which I'd surely soon reap the benefits. I collapsed down on the bed and enveloped myself in the duvet. It was thin and smelly and made me wheeze like a pig.

'This duvet smells horrible,' I said. 'Have you got a clean one?'

He shook his head like an unsecured street sign. 'Sorry,' he said. 'I haven't got a washing machine.'

'Oh, okay, never mind,' I said, hastily steering the conversation away from my obligations as a landlord. 'I'm sure there are lots of good laundrettes around.'

'Actually there aren't,' he said. 'I have to wash my clothes in the -'

'Okay great,' I said. 'I'm glad it's all going well here. But I'm very tired you see, and I do need to go to sleep. Thanks Doorman.'

'Night then,' he grumbled. 'I'll be out here.' I heard his footsteps pad back to the living room, where he turned on the radio and presumably sulked. *You should be grateful for my generosity, Doorman,* I thought. *You should be scattering rose petals across my path.*

I drifted off to sleep and dreamt about Sheena spitting pork scratchings in tenants' faces. Despite her viciousness I missed her companionship. She provided a welcome validatory voice during spells of uncertainty: moments in which I worried we'd validated human rights laws or inflicted genuine distress were happily brushed aside in the name of wealth accumulation. 'They'd shaft us in a heartbeat,' she'd say. 'We need to protect ourselves.' Her words clanged through my dreams and I awoke feeling fortified and confident in the challenge ahead, like a hate preacher enacting the will of some benign and shamefaced god.

The duvet had left me itching terribly, so the next morning I bundled it out of the window and left it curled up in the freezing mud. It was vital he buy a new one, for how else would I achieve comfort the next time I visited?

I emerged into the kitchen and found Doorman eating oats out of a mess tin. 'What's for breakfast, Doorman?' I said. 'Have you got any dragonfruit?'

He pointed to the sack of oats on the countertop. There was a second mess tin beside it, scratched and dented like it'd been salvaged from a bomb trench.

'I'd like an espresso,' I said. 'I'm still quite tired. That mattress is horrible to sleep on.'

'Yes I know,' he said, staring at me expectantly. 'It needs to be replaced.'

Whoops, I thought, realising the implication. 'What I meant was -' I started, hurriedly trying to put a positive spin on my searing back pain. 'I had a lovely sleep. So restful.'

He returned to his cold, dry oats. Bucketing them into his mouth he resembled a clunking rubbish compactor and I had to force myself to remain dispassionate. I reminded myself of Sheena's prescient words: *he'd shaft us in a heartbeat*, and ably disregarded any scraps of sympathy.

I half-filled the tin with oats and sat opposite him at the table. He eyed me with nervous suspicion: was I his friend or his master?

'So, how do you want to do this?' he said.

'I don't know,' I said. 'How are kidnap victims usually rescued? Should we record a charity single?'

'First off we'll need to get inside,' he said, spurred to action. 'Do a sweep of the building. Check the entry points. I'll get the gear sorted.'

'What gear?' I said. 'What do you mean?'

'Bolt cutters, balaclavas, that sort of thing,' he said. 'Essentials for an extraction operation.'

'Oh. Yes. Of course.' I said, genuinely not having

expected such proactivity. 'How come you've got all that equipment? Did you used to be a terrorist?'

'Sort of.' he said.

He finished his oats and rose from the table, breathing swiftly and calmly. He then knelt before a kitchen cupboard. From inside he retrieved the aforementioned bolt cutters and balaclavas, plus binoculars, spray cans, lockpicks and hunting knives. He loaded them into backpacks quickly and cleanly, like an upstanding neighbourhood serial killer, and carried the bags out to the car. 'We'll check the place out this morning, then go back when it's dark,' he said. 'Need to know the layout, vantage points, that sort of thing.'

Blimey, I thought.

We packed ourselves into the car and headed for Crumbford. I sprawled across the back seats and hollered orders, anxious for Doorman not to see me as an equal. I *was* still his master, and couldn't risk a downturn in obedience.

'Give me a cig, Doorman,' I said, noting his Balkan cigs resting by the handbrake. 'I must have a cig now.'

He handed me the packet and I took five, lighting one and pocketing the rest for later use. My head was growing hot and my eyes convulsed as I began to sober up. I sucked the cig frantically, desperately trying to circumvent the hangover that was to crash down on me in five minutes' time. 'I don't feel very well, Doorman,' I said. 'Have you got any whisky?'

'I'm sorry sir, I haven't.' he said. 'Shall we stop at an off licence?'

'Yes, we must,' I said. 'I'm absolutely parched.'

We stopped outside Gladcock's Food & Wine, a crummy little emporium that sold packeted noodles and breast magazines. The proprietors looked hardened by their time behind the counter, their faces haunted patchworks of scars that evinced weekly robberies and spiralling local knife crime.

'A bottle of Warpecker, please.' I said.

He lifted the bottle from the shelf, took my money and didn't say thank you. I returned to the car and guzzled whisky until the pain stopped.

'Better?' said Doorman.

'Yes, a bit,' I said. 'I don't understand why I feel so awful. I only had one or two drinks last night.'

'Sometimes these things happen, sir.' he said, providing no clarity whatsoever.

I lay across the back seats gasping and panting, eagerly chaining cigs in an effort to achieve an equitable level of wellness.

'We're nearly there,' he said, easing the car through a silent zigzag of back streets.

I sat up and finished the remainder of the whisky, absentmindedly hurling the bottle out of the window. It smashed against a bollard and the tinkling glass seemed to awaken the day, intangibly rousing the air around us. I sensed tiny, distant movements in my peripheral vision. Were we being surveilled?

Doorman had halted the car and was scratching in a notepad.

'What are you writing, Doorman?' I said, finishing the last of his cigs. 'And have you got any more cigs?'

'Cameras, alarms, escape routes,' he said. 'Things we'll need to know.'

'Crumbs,' I said. 'Have you done this before?'

'Couldn't say.' he said cryptically. He leaned forwards and backwards in his seat, straining to see up and down the street, high windows, road signs, neighbouring cars.

'Where's number forty-eight?' I said. 'That's the address the bar boy gave me.'

'That one,' he said, nodding at a thoroughly inconspicuous shopfront. Its shutters were down and it was crowned with a tatty plastic canopy adorned with faded Thrushman's branding.

'Are you sure?' I said. 'Isn't that just an old shop?'

'Yes, to the untrained eye,' he said. 'But why would an old shop have five CCTV cameras watching it?'

I looked out of the car window. It took me a while to pick them out but there were, in fact, five cameras trained on the shop: some in plain sight, some nestled behind railings and bolted to walls. 'Why are there so many?' I said.

'Because they don't want anybody going inside.' he said. He started the ignition and drove slowly around the neighbouring streets, gawping like a compromised spy. He stopped suddenly. 'We need to go,' he said. 'We've been seen.'

Before I'd had a chance to confirm this we'd roared off, tearing back towards Crumbford High Street like freewheeling carjackers. I felt drunk and hungover at the same time: my head was thumping while I remained gregariously lucid, barking at Doorman about cigs and CCTV. Terrifyingly, it was only ten o'clock in the morning.

CHAPTER 18

We sat in Doorman's kitchen (my kitchen, really), as he read through his notes. He'd drawn maps and diagrams and seemed to be working out details of the extraction strategy.

'Have you got any painkillers?' I said, floundering even after a three-hour snooze.

He sighed like a petulant footman, rose from the table and retrieved a bottle of aspirin from a kitchen drawer. 'Don't take too many, sir.' he said, inexplicably concerned for my wellbeing. (Presumably he didn't want me to die and leave him homeless.)

I scoffed at his spineless warning and took twelve tablets, washing them down with a fortifying glug of *Murgs*. 'That should do the trick,' I said.

He continued dithering with pencils and I stared about the room, my brain pulsing and zapping like a carnival sideshow. I took in his meagre possessions. His camera sat atop the kitchen counter and was, by some stretch, the most valuable thing he owned. It was a chunky DSLR with a peripheral wide-angle lens, used for photographing idealistic old singers who'd not be admitted to the Ten Hours Club in a million years. It panged my heart a little when I'd later see it seized by zealous bailiffs who'd strip the place of anything of material value.

His clothes, a joyless patchwork of overworn mud rags, were piled in corners, growing rotten from a lack of cupboard space. It appeared he'd salvaged most of them from public rubbish sites, so faded and weatherworn they looked.

There was a nasty little shelving unit against one wall, on which he displayed various trinkets accumulated during a lifetime of thankless drudgery. In pride of place was a framed commendation from the Grotley Miners' Union, awarded for picketing services during the dismantling of the coalmining industry in the 1980s. It would later be deemed valueless by the plundering bailiffs, who'd toss it in a binbag without a second thought.

'Proudest moment of my life, that,' he said, noting my gaze. 'I think we made a real difference.'

You didn't make a scrap of difference, I thought, having experienced first-hand the brassnecked disregard for public wellbeing in the top tiers of government.

'I'm sure you did.' I said, trying not to sound too patronising.

'I've found the house. Here, on the satellite photo,' he said, pointing to a photograph. 'There's a garden at the back - that's our entry point,' he said. 'The cameras are positioned here, here, here, here and here. If we approach from the south -' he traced a line with his finger, 'then we'll avoid the first three. Then we climb over this wall -' he circled a point on the map with a pencil. 'And access the building via the rear entrance.' He looked immeasurably pleased with himself.

'That's the plan?' I said. 'Break in through the back door?'

'That's the best way in.' he said, trying to sound like a commando.

'Fine,' I said, convinced he hadn't the faintest idea what he was doing. 'I'm sure you know what you're doing.'

We waited until evening before venturing out, as Doorman believed the veil of night would significantly reduce our chances of being spotted. 'Trust me.' he said, like a character in a film.

He'd advised I not get roaring drunk before we set off, as such behaviour would likely compromise the operation. His concern was unfounded, of course, as I was a gentle, withdrawn drunk, often retiring to bed after one or two drinks. How could he possibly think I'd fluff things up?

To prove there was nothing to worry about I drank eight cans of *Murgs* and screamed in his face about how calm I was. 'I'm *fine*, can't you see? I'm *fucking fine!*'

At the designated hour he hauled me out to the car and dumped me on the back seat. I was sick immediately, carpeting his footwells in regurgitated bile and choking as I tried to smoke three cigs at once. 'Just try and stay calm,' he said, starting the car. 'We don't want to be seen.'

We purred back into Crumbford and stopped near the back of the building. My skin prickled with cold and I pulled my sleeves over my hands to retain warmth. The night was black and orange, lit by arching street lamps that danced with sweepings of rain.

'Here, put this on.' he said, thrusting a balaclava at me.

Okay Doorman, I said, grateful for the heat it might provide. I yanked it on and immediately felt like a moped-straddling purse snatcher. Might I rob an oligarch's wife?

The horrendous cold had, thankfully, sobered me up, and I clattered out of the car like an unwieldy pile of planks. The dark, pervasive cold swept through my clothes and caused my extremities to tense like frozen prawns.

'This way.' hissed Doorman, gesturing towards an unlit perimeter wall.

I was convinced his plan was doomed but had no choice except to follow him, for no one else had either the tools or the motivation to help me, and there was no way I could do this by myself.

We shuffled along with our backs to the wall. 'Keep still,' he said. 'There's a camera up there.'

He pointed towards a set of railings, on which was

affixed a CCTV camera, grey and blank and staring.

'The back wall's just over there,' he said. 'Hold fire.'

He put his hand on my shoulder like an opportunistic clergyman and made a *ssh*-ing sound. 'Don't move,' he said. 'When I give the signal, run straight towards it.'

The wall was twenty feet from us, black and monolithic in the darkness. There was a thin shackle of barbed wire coiled over it, something Doorman had assured me would be 'no problem,' and which I'd envisaged being far more surmountable than it actually was.

'Go.' he hissed, thumping me in the shoulder. Had he forgotten that I was his lord and master? 'Now.'

I dashed across the glassy black tarmac and reached the wall. I crouched beside it and felt the cold brick through my jumper. For a second I wondered whether Sheena was worth all this hassle. Surely I could get by on my own? I'd done it before and could quite easily do it again. All it'd take was a quick word to Doorman and we'd toss off the balaclavas and thunder back to the Ten Hours for a soothing bottle of Warpecker. I upturned the idea in my head but somehow couldn't bring myself to abandon her.

Doorman checked the street, left then right, and ran across after me. 'Good,' he said. 'Just need to get to the other side.' He unfolded a rope ladder from his backpack and hurled it into the air, snagging one end on a metal stake jutting from the top side of the wall.

'Wait here,' he said, retrieving the boltcutters from his bag. 'I'm going to climb up and cut the wire. When I jump, follow me over.'

'Okay, fine.' I said, already exhausted. I daydreamed about a steaming butterbean casserole and wondered how long it'd be before I could retire to the Pig & Bucket for twenty-five whiskies and three packets of Thrushman's.

He sprung up the ladder and held firm at the top, snapping the barbed wire and exhaling breathy blue swirls. Instinctively I kept lookout, unsure what I'd do if we were interrupted.

The streets were desolate, icy, silent. I could feel the cold around my eyes and mouth where the balaclava was exposed and couldn't stop shivering. How dearly I'd love to be drunk again, I thought, cursing my lamentable sobriety. Is this how normal people felt all the time? Sober and frightened and sad?

Doorman then disappeared over the wall, signalling that I follow him. The rungs of the ladder were light, tubular steel and freezing to the touch, eliciting a burning sensation on the palms of my hands. I skirted up quickly, reached the top and recoiled at the scrabble of barbed wire through which I was expected to crawl. Doorman had alighted on the other side and was pressed flat against the inside wall, breathing quietly and trying not to attract attention. I clambered over the top, snagging my trousers on the sharp, vicious fencing. I prayed for my lambswool to be spared, keeping my arms pinned to my torso in an effort to protect the precious knitwear. I yanked myself through the jagged mesh and clattered down on the other side.

'We made it,' said Doorman, helpfully stating the bloody obvious. 'Now let's get inside.'

The wall surrounded a large, unlit, grassless courtyard. In it were dark palletfuls of medical and computer equipment: defibrillator pads, cables, circuitboards, all wet and knackered in the gusting rain. 'Are they turning her into a robot?' said Doorman, noting the cabling tubes and discarded electrical belts.

'I hope not,' I said. 'Our electricity bill's already through the roof.'

We edged around the perimeter towards the building.

'Stop,' said Doorman. 'Don't move.'

The back door had swung open and a figure emerged from inside. It was a man, though we only saw him in profile. He was tall and solid and lit a cigar, the tip of which glowed like an infected penile head. The thought of cigar smoke caused my stomach to churn and I felt almost ready to vomit. Doorman caught his breath as he heard the growling, squeezing sound resonating from deep inside me: deep and horribly conspicuous, it felt like bile was being pushed in all directions by my cartwheeling guts. Doorman elbowed me in an effort to make it stop but the sick rose in my throat like an overflowing slot drain: pungent and acrid and burning like a swell of hot gravy. The shadowed figure turned in our direction.

'Oh no,' said Doorman. He froze. 'We've been seen.'

The figure was walking towards us, the light of his cigar dancing like a firefly.

'Hello?' he said.

I'd torn off my balaclava and was chundering wretchedly over Doorman's legs.

'Are you okay, old thing?' The cigar neared my face and the owner came into view. It was the juror: his eyes were bloodshot and glassy and he appeared happily tipsy. 'What're you doing out here?'

I manage to stop retching long enough to look at him. 'What do you mean?' I said. Doorman didn't say a word.

'I mean, why are you out here, old chap?' he said. 'Bloody cold, isn't it?'

'Oh, er, yes,' I said. 'Yes it is.'

'Bit worse for wear, old sock?' he laughed, slapping me on the back. 'Sorry to hear that. Happens to us all though, eh? Still a bloody shame. Let's get you back inside, shall we? Get you some coke. Straighten you out.'

I wiped my mouth. Was he really just going to walk us inside? 'Yes, okay,' I said. I gestured to Doorman. 'This is my -' I hesitated, I didn't want to call him a *friend*, but nor could I remember his name. Ray? Roy? 'My colleague.'

The juror extended his hand. 'Evening old chap,' he said. 'Bloody good to meet you. Love the mask.'

Doorman pulled off his balaclava. 'Hello.' he said sheepishly.

The juror tapped cigar ash into a bird feeder. 'You chaps been here a while? I've only just arrived. Been over at the Ten Hours, you see. Wine consultations and so on.'

'Oh. Yes,' I said, somewhat unnerved. 'We've been here all evening.'

'Great stuff,' he said. 'Let's get you back inside then, shall we? It's bloody perishing.'

'Okay,' I said as he snaked his arm around me (so strong!) 'Let's go back in.'

I caught Doorman's eye in a flash of panic: *what are we doing?* I had no idea. What were we walking into?

The juror, jocular and corrupt, led me across the courtyard to the open back door. 'Will you be okay to walk, old sock?' he said.

'Oh yes,' I said. 'I'll be fine.'

I felt an intense kinship with him at this moment. He was, at heart, a fundamentally bad person, yet had nothing but warmth and compassion for those he considered friends. I felt oddly guilty: I couldn't help but feel I might be cutting some significant ties by breaking Sheena out of her prison. But what if it wasn't a prison? What if they'd simply enrolled her on a college course or residential spa break? I'd certainly not want to obstruct her learning or physical wellbeing by barrelling in unannounced. Should we turn back?

'After you, old thing.' said the juror, ushering me over the threshold.

Inside was dimly lit, with purple striplights illuminating the cluttered passageway. It felt warm and neutral like an electrical shop and was notable for its disorientating silence. Was there nobody else here?

'You lead the way old chap.' he said.

I panicked, clueless as to where I was expected to go. The walls were thickly carpeted and my footsteps were silent as I stumbled ahead, blindly following the corridor.

'So what's your game then, old thing?' The juror said to Doorman.

'He's my chauffeur,' I said, hoping to avoid any talk about socialism. 'He drives me around.'

'Good solid work that,' said the juror. 'My grandfather used to drive SS men around. You know, during the war.'

Doorman, clearly horrified, said nothing.

'Oh right,' I said. 'What was that like?'

'He enjoyed it,' he said. 'And there were a few perks for the family, of course.'

'What kind of perks?' I said, still fumbling through the darkness.

'Gold, paintings, that sort of thing. He knew where it was all hidden, you see. Used to drive them to the hideouts and so on. Certainly set us in good stead.'

I ummed and aahed, now petrified. 'He sounds very resourceful.' I managed.

'Yes I suppose so,' said the juror. 'I miss him sometimes, the old sod. Didn't hear much from him after Nuremberg, to be honest. That's probably what got me interested in the law game in the first place.'

Mercifully, I had to cut short the conversation as I was about to be sick again.

'Are you alright, old chap?' he said. 'Shall we get you to the lav?'

I nodded frantically as my cheeks swelled with vomit.

'Come on then, you lead the way.'

Problematically, I had no idea where I was going.

'Maybe better if you go first,' said Doorman, hoisting me up. 'He's a bit worse for wear.'

'Right you are, old thing,' said the juror. 'Follow me, chaps.'

He led us up a flight of stairs and past a door with a frosted glass window.

'What's in there?' said Doorman, wisely acting as our shared mouthpiece.

'Oh, er, nothing for you to worry about, old chap,' said the juror, shooting me a look that said *he shouldn't be here*. 'Just cupboards, that sort of thing.'

At the top of the stairs was a cramped little door, presumably the bathroom, and Doorman unhanded me.

'Will you be okay, old horse?' said the juror, half stumbling back down the stairs.

'Yes,' I said, 'I just need a few minutes if that's okay.'

'Of course, old chap, of course. See you in the basement, okay?'

Yes, okay I said, fearful of what awaited us in the basement.

He skittered off and Doorman and I bolted ourselves into the toilet.

'What's going on here?' I said. 'Where the hell are we?'

'I don't know,' he said, mopping sweat off his forehead. 'But I'm pretty sure this is where we'll find Sheena.'

'But I thought they only kidnapped vulnerables?' I said. 'Why on earth would they take Sheena? She owns so much property.'

'Maybe they thought she was a liability,' he said. 'She does get angry very quickly.'

'Maybe,' I said. 'Either way, we need to get her out of here.'

'Okay,' he said. 'Shall we go down?'

I nodded my assent and we eased open the bathroom door. The landing was silent and we creaked down the stairs to the floor below.

'You should probably go ahead of me,' I said, pointing him towards the dark, plunging staircase. 'You've done this type of thing before.'

Quite obviously terrified but unwilling to lose face, Doorman began his slow descent. I followed him closely, reasoning that anything terrible we encountered would impact him first, leaving me to turn and run like a military deserter. We edged down the stairs, step by step, our feet padding on the matted carpet. I stared absentmindedly into the gloom, at the sullied wallpaper, the chipped cornicing, and wondered how long the place had been used as a hostage repository. Wouldn't a warehouse or aircraft hangar have made a more convenient prison? Doorman stopped suddenly. It appeared we'd reached the bottom.

146

'What can you see?' I whispered.

'Not a lot,' he said, sarky idiot. 'It's dark.'

We were in a small, sparse little hallway even blacker than the floors above. The ceiling was oppressively low and the carpet had frayed off halfway down the staircase, leaving a dark granite floor that seemed to physically absorb light.

'Is this the basement?' I said. 'Where is everybody?'

'It's so quiet,' he said. 'Where could they all be?'

We edged up the passageway and arrived at a door, black besides a thin glowing outline.

'You should probably go in first,' I said, gesturing him forward.

He stared at me. 'But they don't trust me,' he said. 'Did you see the way that juror looked at me?'

'That's true,' I said. 'But you're more experienced than me. You used to be a terrorist. If anything goes wrong you can throw a bomb at them or something.'

He looked at me. He seemed frightened. 'Okay,' he said. 'Stay close.'

'Alright.' I said, with absolutely no intention of putting myself in harm's way.

He gripped the door handle and eased it open. 'It's locked.' he said, rattling the latch.

'You need to push it harder,' I said. 'Imagine it's a communist bunker.'

He barged the door with his side, grunting slightly. 'No good.' he said.

We froze as the handle suddenly moved from the other side. Someone knew we were here. 'Now *now*.' came an unnervingly familiar voice.

We stood in silence, gripped by fear.

The lock rattled and the door squeaked open. Before us stood Lord Wretchley, hefty and glowering. He was in his shirtsleeves, spritzed with sweat and wielding a lengthy shock prod. 'How did you get in?' he said, his characteristic jocularity now entirely absent. 'You shouldn't be here.'

I knew then that we were in trouble. We were in the bowels of the building, the dark gut in which evil festered like flesh flies, and we were trapped. I had no idea what to say. Should I apologise? Wallop him? 'Is Sheena here?' I mumbled.

He shifted his head and winced. 'You can't have her,' he said. 'We need her.'

His moustache, once analogous to a patriarchal old sheepdog, now appeared as a terrifying slick on the face of a ravenous torturemaster.

'What do you mean?' I stammered. 'Let us in.'

He seemed to have expanded, somehow occupying more square footage than I remembered. He swung the shock prod in loping circles. 'I can't do that I'm afraid,' he said, rubbing his eye with a plump pink hand. 'We're right in the middle of something. Very important -'

He was immediately knocked sideways, thumping into the door and hurling his port and lemon into the air. It'd only taken a second: Doorman had lunged forward and hooked his arm around Wretchley's back, snapping it backwards and flinging him off balance like an errant sack of potatoes. He lay against the doorframe, plump and unconscious.

Doorman grabbed the shock prod. 'Follow me,' he hissed. 'Quickly.'

We dashed past Wretchley's squashed body and into a cavernous, dimly lit beer hall. Its walls were uneven and salty and the ceiling was enormous: arched and cathedralic like the belly of a whale. A rusty balcony ran the perimeter of the room, forming a viewing platform halfway up the length of the western wall. It was here that the patrons were gathered, for we could hear the cacophonous rabble of echoed chatter and see banknotes being tossed over the balcony edge.

The ground floor of the room, roughly twenty feet below, was divided into sixty-four black and white tile squares, each the size of a manhole cover. Standing on the squares, in a seemingly unpatternable sequence, were people. Real people. They were barely alive: their eyes were half-closed and their skin drained of humanity, crumbly like premium Roquefort. Some stood in rows while others were dotted illogically about the grid. Then I saw their faces. Faces I recognised. Mrs Muggins. She stood like a zombie, statuesque on a corner square with her arms snapped to her sides like thin, brittle stalks. The bar boy was near the centre of the grid, his face lopsided as his insentient features seemed to slip away from his head. He looked bruised and thrashed and the dog collar around his neck was studded with bite marks. Then I saw Sheena. She was on an outlying gridline, standing on a black square, staring deeply into nothingness. The only time I'd seen her so vegetative was during our life-threatening ouzo binge, when she'd blacked out and hyperventilated until her respiratory system failed. Among the other figures I recognised was a journalist from outside the courthouse, one of our swindled man tenants, a security guard from the marmalade factory and the local market lady who sold sausages out of a hardpan rust bucket. Disappointingly there was no sign of Ed.

'What the hell is this?' I whispered to Doorman.

Doorman shook his head. 'I don't know. It looks like some kind of game.'

We needed to hide. Despite the low visibility we were exposed to the sightlines of the balcony revellers and would surely be spotted in a matter of moments.

'This way.' said Doorman, ushering me towards a small bar adjacent to the door through which we'd entered. I crouched behind him and we scuttled towards it.

We stopped behind the bar and peeked over the top. We heard drunken bellowing from high on the balcony, thuggish howls for Wretchley to 'get a move on.'

'Hurry up, you old bastard!' they hooted, hurling glasses over the edge. 'It's our turn!' I noticed the distant outline of the juror, flanked by the health secretary and various luminaries I recognised from the Ten Hours.

'Seriously, what are they talking about?' I said, ducking back behind the bar.

Doorman had replaced his balaclava and advised I did the same. He was studying the configuration of the people on the grid. 'They're playing chess,' he said, staring at me in terror. 'Human chess.'

I assumed I'd misheard due to the muffling effects of the balaclava. 'What did you say?'

'Look,' he said. 'See how they're arranged?'

I peered over the top of the bar. Worryingly, it seemed he was right. Upon closer inspection I saw the prisoners were arranged in deliberate geometric patterns, positioned as if by some omnipotent strategist.

'What the bloody hell's going on?' crowed the overhead rabble. 'We've not got all night, old man.'

'They're going to notice something's up,' said Doorman. 'We need to move quickly. Can you see Sheena?'

'Sort-of.' I said. From my vantage point she was partly obscured by the local street performer whose sudden disappearance had prompted a citywide dancing ban. 'She's on the far side.'

'We're going to need to make a dash for it,' he said. 'There's no other way. Run out there, grab her, then back up the stairs.'

'What if they see us?' I said. The intoxicated rabble were beginning to notice their chess game had stopped and were peering over the balcony, looking for Wretchley.

'We've just got to hope we can get out before they get down here.'

I nodded. 'Okay.' I said.

I took a deep breath.

'Go.' he said.

We dashed out from behind the bar, across the giant chessboard towards Sheena. We were quickly spotted by the overhanging throng, who pelted us with bottles and glassware.

'Hey! Stop, scum!' they bellowed, hurling truffle platters at our heads.

We ducked and lurched among the statuesque captives, bumping into them without eliciting even a squeak. They were so zapped they didn't even notice us, staring blankly at the walls with the stoic emptiness of credit controllers.

Our shoes squeaked on the floor tiles, the sharp sound reverberating about the hall like symphonic bird chatter.

'Grab them!' came shouts from overhead. We heard the clattering rumble of brogues as the members rushed down the stairs to stop us.

'Pick her up,' said Doorman as we approached Sheena. 'Quickly!'

I took her head while he held her legs, and we raced back towards the exit. The members had reached the ground floor now, and were spilling out onto the tile floor like baby spiders. We reached the basement door and I banged it open with Sheena's head, relieved she'd feel no pain in her current state of stupefaction. We yanked the door shut behind us, avoiding the marauders' clutches by a whisker. Back in the passageway we roared up to the ground floor and back out to the courtyard.

'This way,' hissed Doorman, yanking the rope ladder from his backpack. He tossed it over the wall and pulled it taut. We could hear pounding from the staircase behind us. The members would be on us in a matter of seconds. We squirmed and wobbled up the ladder, balancing Sheena's body between us as we miraculously vaulted the wall. My precious lambswool was shredded by the barbed wire, flaying about me in soft, mangled strings.

'Are you over?' said Doorman.

I told him I was, and dropped to the street on the other side. I held Sheena like a drunken dance partner, half-dragging her towards the car while cradling her back with the crook of my arm. Doorman had reached the top of the wall but the club members had caught up with him. He was kicking and thrashing as they tried dragging him back into the courtyard, slavering like rabid hellhounds. It seemed he was struggling and he lost his footing, flailing comically before finding his grip on the barbed wire.

Would he be killed? It wouldn't be a *huge* loss (he paid minimal rent) but I wasn't able to drive and it was a perishing evening. I *needed* him alive. His arms flapped as they dragged him downwards. Then I remembered the shock prod. Wretchley's shock prod. Presumably used for moving the 'pieces' on the chess board.

'Shock prod!' I bellowed, immensely proud of my resourcefulness. Might I receive a Royal Marine's commendation?

He looked in my direction, first confused, then clear. He yanked it out of his belt loop and zapped the members one by one, dispersing them like bothersome toads. Once safe, he scrambled down the outer wall and retracted the rope ladder. He dashed towards me and threw open the car door. 'Get her in the back,' he said. 'Make sure she's breathing.'

I tossed Sheena across the back seat and clambered inside while Doorman started the car.

We roared off, through the freezing nighttime and back towards the safety of the town. The bellowing dissipated and all I heard was the rattle of the car on the tarmac.

'Have you got any cigs?' I said, unable to think of anything else to say.

He shook his head, staring at the road. He seemed disquieted.

'Are you okay?' I said, slightly miffed he'd not asked after my wellbeing.

'Let's just get her home,' he said. 'We can talk about it then.'

Fine, I thought, sorry I'd wasted my compassion on him.

We drove for miles through freezing, inky blackness,

idly counting the spots of rain on the windscreen and intermittently checking Sheena was still alive. What had they *done* to her?

CHAPTER 19

Sheena lay in bed for a week, unspeaking and gaunt. She was generally unresponsive, groaning and cursing with all the muster her debilitation allowed. She was unable to grip cigs with her hands, meaning I had to administer them puff by puff, bent over her bed like a reluctant set square.

I'd tried extracting information about her capture but none was forthcoming. She'd bark sporadic, chess-related words and phrases ('rook 5!', 'bad bishop!') before glazing over and gesturing to the glass of brandy I kept topped up by the bedside.

Doorman had stayed with us for several nights, ostensibly for protection but mostly for a dry place to sleep. He slept on the sofa, snuffling like a malnourished reptile under cheap and threadbare bedding. Originally I'd given him the spare duvet, a premium goosedown comforter that'd cost more than Aunt Loz's euthanasia treatment, but he'd sullied it with pubic shavings so I'd palmed him off with a sackcloth filched from the utility cupboard.

He seemed to be suffering some kind of post-traumatic shock, given the screams I'd hear from the living room while trying to sleep. After two nights I had to stuff a sock into his mouth to shut him up, so bloodcurdling were his shrieks. When I asked what was wrong, he claimed he was doing 'vocal exercises' in preparation for a political agitators' conference at which he was due to address a mudpatch of deluded tub-thumpers.

At the end of the first week, after administering medicine Doorman had reassured me would perk her up, Sheena became lucid. She managed to sit up in bed and, much to the relief of my carpal bones, was able to grip cigs. 'Rent.' she said, her first words in seven days. 'Rent.'

'It's okay,' I soothed. 'Ed's still paying his rent.'

'Thank God,' she said, reaching for a Thrushman's. 'What about the other tenants?'

'They've been paying too,' I said. 'No change there.'

Suddenly, like an unclogged gutpipe, she burst into tears.

'What on earth's the matter?' I said. 'Is there something wrong with your cig?'

'No,' she sobbed. 'It's a lovely cig. Feels like I've not had a proper cig for hours.'

Don't mind if I do, I thought, plucking a Thrushman's from the packet.

She continued: 'I just feel a bit overwhelmed.'

By now Doorman had heard us blething and was knocking gently on the bedroom door.

Sheena tensed. 'Who's that?' she said, pulling the duvet over her face. 'A cabinet minister?' She was as white as an indie band, terrified beyond recognition.

'It's okay,' I said. 'It's only Doorman. He's been staying here. Keeping guard.'

'Who's watching the flats?' she said, still shaking.

'No one,' I said. 'But I'm sure they're fine. It's just the students and the old woman. They'll be okay for a few days unguarded.'

'Okay,' she said. 'Sorry. I'm just a bit spooked. Go on, let him in.'

I opened the door and beckoned Doorman inside. 'She's awake,' I whispered. 'Those pills must've worked.'

He nodded and approached the bed. 'Hi Sheena,' he

said. 'Are you okay?'

'Hi Doorman,' she said. 'Have you paid your rent this month?'

'Oh, er -' he faltered, presumably having expected praise.

'Just make sure it's paid on time,' she said, gently closing her eyes. 'Now get back to the flats.'

'Oh,' he said. 'Yes. Of course.' He hesitated, pulling at his neckskin. 'Could I just ask you a few questions? Find out what happened?'

Sheena flapped at him with an outstretched arm. 'Just get out.' she said. She looked at me, her eyes cold and pleading. 'Get rid of him,' she said. 'What's he even doing here anyway? Shouldn't he be out catching squirrels or something?'

I cocked my head empathetically at Doorman. 'Might be best if you go,' I said, as gently as a grievance counsellor. 'I'll help you collect your rags and so on.'

We exited to the living room and I assisted in retrieving his horrible clothes from the sofa (crinkly bedsocks, soiled gut vests) and tossed them into the holdall he'd brought with him.

'Okay, bye then.' I said, wondering if I should thank him. He didn't really *do* much to aid in Sheena's rescue besides drive the car, and I could've done that without even holding a licence (all you needed was to waggle the pedals and fondle the gear knob).

He packed up his junk and headed for the door. 'Good job, comrade,' he said. 'Mission accomplished.'

'Oh yes, of course,' I said, my bones crushed in a pummelling handshake. 'Good job.'

He left; a slumped, sorry figure traipsing down the corridor in a building he once guarded like a loyal beefeater. Should I pity him? I wasn't sure. I needed to consult Sheena.

I sat in her leather recliner drinking *Murgs* while she sipped brandy in her sickbed.

'Do you remember what happened?' I said. 'Do you know where they took you?'

'I remember being at the Ten Hours,' she said. 'Then getting in a car. Wretchley gave me a drink. Then it all goes blank. That's it.'

'Oh.' I said, slightly unsure how to explain what'd happened.

'I must've been *hammered*,' she said. 'Did he drop me off here? I vaguely remember being in a car.'

It was becoming troublingly clear that she had no recollection whatsoever of her incarceration. 'Do you remember being in a beer hall?' I said, hoping to jolt some synaptic activity.

'When?' she said. 'Recently?'

'Fairly recently.' I said.

'Not at all. Did we go there after the Ten Hours?'

'Well, sort of,' I said. 'You certainly did. You don't remember anything at all?'

She was becoming impatient. Why was I being so coy? Did I, in some way, *enjoy* being the storyteller?

'Nothing at all,' she said. 'Seriously, what the hell happened?'

I relayed the long, ungainly story of how she'd been kidnapped, drugged and used as a human chess piece for the entertainment of corrupt parliamentarians.

'Is this a joke?' she said, once I'd brought her up to speed. 'Are you pulling my pud?'

'Unfortunately not,' I said. 'Isn't it awful?'

Without missing a beat she hurled her glass at the wall, showering me with splinters and shards. 'Fuck!' she screamed, ripping out the desklamp and flinging it at the wall. 'Fuck, shit, FUCK!'

I dashed from the room and yanked the door shut behind me. I stood nervously outside as she tore the place to pieces, wincing as glass crashed and tinkled. Wood splintered and plaster cracked as her rage unfurled like a payday riot. Thankfully we owned the property so there

157

was no deposit against which to charge the damage, yet still I felt a knaw of unease. What if the neighbours reported us to the freehold committee? I quickly regained my composure, however, remembering the building was empty and the other apartments were used primarily to bury corporate slush funds. (One noteworthy tycoon owned the residence downstairs and used it to make bestial porn films starring a gun dog named Munroe.)

The destruction ceased and the bedroom door fell open. Sheena emerged, panting and red as beef tongue. 'They have to pay for this,' she said. 'I'm going to make them pay.'

That'll never happen, I thought, aware of how utterly invincible they were. 'Oh, okay,' I said. 'How would you do that?'

'I don't know yet,' she said. 'But I'll think of something. We're going to destroy them.'

I felt uncomfortable being included in her scheme. Despite their obvious wrongdoing I enjoyed the group and the social cache its membership afforded us. 'Maybe we should just forget about it,' I said. 'You might feel different in a couple of days.' Unfortunately I knew for a fact she'd never feel different. She'd chase this to the grave.

'We'll start tomorrow.' she said, uncorking an unctuous Chablis.

CHAPTER 20

Sheena's vengeful murmurings, vague and admirable as they seemed, would ultimately come to nothing, and for one very specific reason.

The previous night we'd drunk a case of Chablis and made prank calls to hospices before collapsing in our own urine. We'd awoken to a ringing phone (Sheena later suggested we cut off all communication with the outside world), that I answered with a head like an exploded nail bomb. 'Hello?' I croaked.

'Where've you been?' said Stu, robbed of his characteristic exuberance.

I couldn't find the strength to explain it all to him, so instead lied like a rail boss. 'We've been away,' I said. 'Cyanide fishing.'

'Right,' he said, clearly disbelieving of my nonsense. 'Whatever. We've got a problem.'

'Who's on the phone?' said Sheena, having woken up and vomited into a plug socket.

'It's Stu,' I said. 'He's says there's a problem.'

'There's always a problem,' she said. 'Tell him I got kidnapped and used as a chess piece.'

I returned to the call, my brain throbbing like a pustule. 'Sorry,' I said. 'What's the problem?'

'It's Ed,' said Stu. 'He's awake.'

I exhaled, my chest rattling from a million Thrushman's. 'Is he okay?' I said, dearly hoping he'd lost his sight or his continence or something.

'He's groggy,' he said. 'But he's lucid.' He paused. 'And he's angry.'

I said nothing. Should I just hang up?

'Are you still there?' he said.

'Yes,' I groaned, my head convulsing in pain. 'You said Ed's angry.'

'He is. He holds you personally responsible for his ordeal. And he wants to sue.'

I yawned. *This again.* 'Just call Hilary Bell,' I said. 'He'll sort it out.'

'I did,' said Stu. 'He wants nothing to do with you.'

'That can't be right.' I said. Was Stu being deliberately facetious? 'He's our lawyer. He looks after this kind of thing.'

Stu said nothing, presumably busy concocting further ways to ruin my morning. 'Look,' he said, with a firmness that caused me another involuntary erection. 'Hilary Bell won't answer my calls. He's not returning messages. He's ditched you. Have you done anything to piss him off?'

'That's rubbish,' I said. 'You were probably just phoning the wrong number. I'll give you the right number and you can try again.' He huffed out an exasperated sigh, somehow implying I was being unreasonable. *Do as you're told, Stu*, I thought, irritated at his insubordination. Hadn't we netted him two hefty commissions? Why wasn't he begging to tug me off?

'Listen,' he said. 'I'm done. I can't keep doing this. I'm an estate agent, not your PA.'

Sheena had padded into the kitchen and seemed impatient. 'What's going on?' she said, lighting two cigs.

'Hilary Bell won't answer Stu's calls.' I said.

'Probably got the wrong number,' she said. 'Tell him to try again.'

'Tell her I'm not trying again,' came Stu's voice in my

ear. 'This isn't part of my job.'

'Here, look,' said Sheena. 'Here's his number.' She thrust a business card at me. 'Tell him to phone that. Easy.'

'Listen,' said Stu, 'I can hear you. And I'm not phoning anyone. I've got a job to do.'

'Sorry, what?' I said, having ignored him completely. I took the card from Sheena. 'His number's 0-2-1-6 -' The line went dead. Surely he hadn't hung up on me?

'What's he saying?' said Sheena, smoke cascading from her mouth like candyfloss.

'He hung up on me.' I said.

'What?' she said. 'Just then? He hung up on you?'

'Yes.' I said, wincing as my nerve endings fizzed and spasmed.

'But he's an estate agent,' she said. 'We should be the ones hanging up on him. It was probably a mistake with the telegraph poles or something. Call him back.'

'You're right,' I said. 'There's most likely a problem with the sky wires. I'll phone him back.'

I dialled Stu's office and was greeted by a fellow estate agent who told me he wasn't available. 'There was a problem with the telegraph poles,' I explained, adjusting my reptilian scrotum (it'd weathered badly over the years, now resembling a leathery old rock bag.) 'Please put Stu on the phone.'

The second estate agent, evidently a seasoned liar (weren't they all?), claimed he'd love to pass the phone over but unfortunately Stu was on another call. However, an exciting new property had just come across his desk - would we like to arrange a viewing?

'What?' I said.

'What's he saying?' snapped Sheena. 'Is he phoning Hilary Bell?'

'This house has *literally* just hit the market,' said the estate agent. 'I'd strongly recommend seeing it sooner rather than later.'

161

'Hang on, liar,' I said, covering the phone receiver with my palm. I turned to Sheena. 'Someone else answered,' I said. 'He wants us to see a house.'

'What's the resale value?'

'I can tell you guys are interested,' said the estate agent, his voice muffled. 'Shall we say today at three o'clock?'

'No, no, stop,' I said. 'Just give the phone to Stu. We need to talk to him about our lawyer, Hilary Bell. Do you know Hilary Bell?'

'I'd love to,' he said. 'But he's on another call right now. In the meantime, shall we firm up a date for this viewing?'

'What's going on?' said Sheena, jabbing a finger at the phone.

I don't know, I mouthed hopelessly.

'Give it to me.' she said.

Thank heavens, I thought, lighting three Thrushman's as I was absolved of all responsibility.

'Hello?' said Sheena. 'Yes, I heard. What's the resale value?'

A pause.

'Nope, too low,' she said. 'Stop wasting our time, liar. Put Stu on the phone. No, I don't care if he's on another call. Put him on the phone. Put him on the phone you piece of dirt!'

Her face was as red as Dad's credit rating. Was she going to suggest we visit Stu's office? 'If you don't put him on the phone we're going to come to your office and speak to him ourselves,' she said. Another pause. 'Fine. See you soon, liar.'

She hung up and hurled the phone off the balcony. It cracked to pieces on a neighbours' car windscreen. 'We need to go to their office,' she said. 'Stu's trying to dodge us.'

'Maybe we should try phoning Hilary Bell first,' I said, dreading the thought of leaving the house with a head full of pulped scorpions. 'Just to make sure.'

'Yes, okay,' she said. 'Maybe you're right. Stu's probably

just got the wrong number. Can we use your phone?'

Fine, I thought, begrudgful of wasting my precious contract minutes.

The phone rang and rang. No answer.

'He's not there,' I said. 'Shall I leave a message?'

'Let me do it.' said Sheena, snatching the phone away. I hoped she'd not throw it out of the window, for how else would I access titillating chatlines?

'Hilary Bell, it's Sheena. Answer your bloody phone. We need you to sort Ed out. He's awake and he wants to sue us. Phone me back on this number you gangly prick.'

She hung up and tossed me the phone. 'That should do it,' she said. 'Firm but fair.'

We didn't hear from Hilary Bell for two days, at which point we decided to call again. Still no answer. We phoned twenty more times with no result.

'What's going on?' I said. 'Should we complain to the telephone exchange?'

'No point,' said Sheena. 'They'd just laugh at you and call you a spud. We need to get down to his office. Show our faces.'

Was I a spud? I hoped not. 'Okay,' I said. 'Let's do that.'

Too good for the bus, we phoned Doorman to demand a lift.

'He owes us, big time.' said Sheena.

Does he? I raised an uncomprehending eyebrow.

'Course he does,' she said. 'He ruined our goosedown comforter. Got pubes all over it.'

'Oh,' I said. 'Yes, maybe you're right.'

Her rationale followed that given his sorrowful income (occasional mudpints in exchange for political canvassing) he'd not be able to replace the duvet in a timely fashion, and had thus sank further into our debt.

'I'll grab a cashmere,' she said. 'You get him round here.'

I dialled Doorman's number and waited. No answer. What could possibly be more important than our transportation requirements? His answerphone clicked on. 'Doorman, it's me,' I said, tired of our calls being ducked. 'We need a lift. Bring your car round immediately. Okay. Bye.'

A minute later the phone rang.

'Hello?'

'Hi there.' said Doorman. He sounded blearier than usual. Had he been making mail bombs?

'Did you get my message?' I said. 'We need a lift. Come round here immediately.'

'Okay,' he said, somewhat cagily. 'But can I use your bath?'

'Our bath?' I said. 'What for? Are you making vodka? For communists?'

He paused. His breathing was slow and strained. 'I just need a bath.' he said.

I told him that was fine, even though I knew Sheena would object irascibly to the idea. I just needed him to get here. There then followed a knock at the door. Who could this possibly be? Brush salesmen?

'Hello?' I said. 'Who's there? Stu? Wretchley?'

'It's me,' said Doorman. 'Can I still use the bath?'

I opened the door. He stood before me, smelling like a litter tray and breathing like a tumble drier.

'How did you get here so quickly?' I said. 'Weren't we just talking on the phone?'

'Yes,' he said, his jowls hanging loose and stubbled around his collar. 'I've been sleeping in the car park.'

'Who's at the door?' yelled Sheena. 'Tell them to piss off. We're leaving in a minute.'

'It's Doorman,' I said. 'Apparently he's been sleeping in the car park.'

'What?' she said, joining us at the door. 'Why aren't you sleeping at the flats, Doorman? Are you trying to get a rent discount? Because you're paying very little as it is. In fact I think it's time you had an increase.'

'I couldn't get into the flats,' he said. 'Since you

changed the locks. I didn't want to mention it in case you got angry and raised the rent.'

'What do you mean?' she said. 'Changed the locks? Who's changed the locks?'

'I thought you did,' he said. 'My key doesn't work. Who else would've done it?'

Sheena begun boiling like a panful of cabbage. 'Bastards,' she said. 'Those *bastards.*'

'What do you mean?' I said, quietly thick. 'Who would've changed our locks?'

'Can't you guess?' she said. 'Wretchley, the juror, the health secretary - one of them's got a key to the building. They're trying to take it back.'

'No, they wouldn't do that, would they?' I said.

She looked at me quizzically. 'You two zapped them with a shock prod.' she said, so droll I thought her larynx would collapse. 'They're not our friends anymore.'

'We were rescuing you.' said Doorman, still cloyingly eager for praise.

'Why didn't you just leave me there?' she said. 'I was fine! I had free drugs, I was numb -'

'But you weren't *free!*' he said.

'It doesn't matter!' she said. 'I felt nothing. For the first time in my life I felt nothing. Do you know what that's like?'

Immediately I felt ratified. I'd been against the rescue operation from the beginning, charmed into submission by Doorman's urban guerrilla schtick. How could he have done this to poor Sheena?

'But we still need a lift,' she said. 'So let's go. We can sort this out later.'

We shuffled down to his car and I felt the power dynamic realigning. Doorman was no longer an equal, nor even a sidekick, but once again the subordinate grunt at whom we'd pelted kitchen debris.

'Where are your cigs?' said Sheena, idly scratching the car window with a house key. 'I need cigs.'

Doorman passed over a packet of Balkan cigarettes (apparently his contact was now sleeping with the son of a warlord, meaning his supply was effectively limitless). 'Help yourselves.' he said.

We arrived at Plugwood Broadway and told Doorman to park his car out of sight. 'We can't compromise our position by being seen in this shitheap,' said Sheena. 'There's no way he'll take us seriously.'

'Okay then,' he said, looking sad and dejected. 'I'll head down Ratmouth Street. There's a bin store there I can park behind.'

'Do whatever you want,' said Sheena, leaving the car door open. 'Just stay out of our way.'

He drove off at a maudlin pace, his exhaust pipe rattling like Sheena's one lung. I couldn't escape the grip of sympathy as I caught his downturned face rounding the corner. Was he crying? I told myself I didn't care a jot and the only reason I felt anything was because I didn't want his tears soddening the cig supply.

We buzzed Hilary Bell's office and were, somewhat predictably, ignored.

'Press all of them,' said Sheena. 'Someone will let us in.'

I hammered every button on the panel, some with staccatoed fervour, others with a droning persistence.

'Keep going,' she said. 'They can't ignore us forever.'

I buzzed until my fingers ached.

'Who's there?' came a voice. 'Stop pressing our bell.'

'Let us in,' said Sheena. 'We need to see our lawyer.'

'Who are you?'

'None of your business,' she said, spitting blood at the intercom (did she have bronchitis?) 'Let us in.'

Fascinatingly, the door then unlatched. We were in. We arrived at Hilary Bell's door and hammered even more aggressively. I felt a strange loping in my guts, a mercurial thrill I imagined one experienced prior to a firm, robust car crash. I was *enjoying* this.

'Open up, Hilary Bell!' roared Sheena. 'We need to

speak to you!'

I rattled the handle but the door was tightly sealed.

'Why won't you answer our calls?' she bellowed, thumping hard on the polished wood. 'You're supposed to be our lawyer.'

The door then unlocked from the other side. It eased open a crack, revealing a sliver of Hilary Bell. 'Go home,' he said. 'Don't come back here.'

His voice was stern yet tremulous, with an almost imperceptible waver. It was noticeable only because his usual timbre was so unassailable; a voice that could charm the birds from the trees and hand them life sentences in the same breath.

Sheena tried to wedge her foot in the door. 'Let us in, Hilary Bell,' she said. 'We're your clients and we demand to speak to our lawyer.'

'Go away,' he said, fixing us with a haunted stare. 'I can't see you anymore. Goodbye.'

He snapped the door shut.

'What was that?' said Sheena, rapping irritably at the door with her knuckles.

'He seemed strange,' I said. 'Why didn't he open the door?'

'Something's not right,' she said, refuelled with purpose after a Thrushman's and a coughing fit. 'Something weird's going on.'

I agreed.

'They know we can't defend ourselves in court. That we're screwed without Hilary Bell.'

'Maybe we should buy some Warpecker,' I said. 'I'm thirsty from all this stress.'

'Good thinking,' she said, barrelling down the stairs. 'Let's head home and plan our next move. We're going to need to find a new solicitor from somewhere.'

We strode from the building and back down Ratmouth Street, an unremarkable byway famous only for the pauper beheadings that happened in the 1860s.

'Where did he say he was parked?' she said. 'I barely even listen to his prattle anymore.'

'He said he'd be by a bin store.' I said.

'The whole place looks like a bin to me,' she said. 'Shit everywhere.'

We continued to the end of the street and arrived in a gravelled turnout.

'Isn't that -' I said.

'His car,' she said. 'Idiot's just left it there. Where the hell is he? St. Petersburg?'

The car was parked beside a rusted iron gate, behind which stood wheelie bins groaning with rubbish. The driver's door was open and the engine sputtered softly. We peered inside. A cig lay burning in the footwell and the stereo crackled with anti-capitalist rhetoric.

'Don't mind if I do.' said Sheena, nabbing the cig and taking a hearty pull.

'Where is he?' I said.

'Probably urinating.' she said, exhaling into the frost.

'You're probably right.' I said.

We waited for three minutes before growing furious. 'Seriously, who does he think he is?' she shrieked, booting the car as hard as she could. 'We need to get home!'

I'd climbed into the driver's seat in an effort to keep warm but the heater had conked out years ago. 'Maybe he's taking photographs of dustbins.' I said. 'Or he could be making a phone call.' This was a ridiculous suggestion given his pitifully meagre social circle.

'Good one.' she said, loudly gargling phlegm.

I dug into my pockets and tried to glean warmth from my cable knit. Time ticked on. Six minutes. Seven minutes.

'This is torture,' said Sheena. 'Eight minutes he's kept us waiting now. Absolute bastard. I can't wait to evict him. Honestly, I'm going to make sure all his mining trophies, or whatever the hell they are, are melted down and made into shackles to keep service workers chained to their floor mops. He'll curse the day he left us out here to freeze.'

I nodded in vague agreement, wondering whether she was just angry or had in fact tipped into the realms of madness. Twelve minutes. Fifteen minutes. My head was resting on the dashboard now, my tongue cracked and appetent. 'This is the longest I've ever had to wait for anything,' I said. 'I think I'm going to faint from the thirst.'

'Me too,' said Sheena, hacking phlegm into the tapedeck. 'We need to get home *right now*.'

I bumped my forehead off the steering wheel. Then an idea hit me. 'How difficult is it to drive?' I said, idly clicking the indicators. The engine was running and the keys hung coyly from the ignition.

'It's probably not that hard,' she said, presumptuously climbing into the passenger seat. 'Doorman could drive, and he was as thick as a pudding bowl.'

'That's true.' I said, despite suspecting he was actually rather bright.

'Apparently even babies can drive in some countries.'

Did she genuinely believe half the things she said?

'Blimey.' I mustered.

'Why don't you give it a go?'

I hesitated.

'Just press the pedals and waggle the gearknob around. Anyone can do that.'

'Maybe you're right,' I said. 'If Doorman can do it then can't be that difficult.'

'Exactly,' she said. 'Come on then, get us home.'

I bowed down on the accelerator and the car revved uncertainly.

'Should it move?' I said, revving the pedal again.

'I don't know,' said Sheena. 'Try one of the other pedals. See what they do.'

I pressed the pedals like a rock guitarist, hoping by some miracle they'd propel the car forward. 'Nothing's happening,' I said. 'Should we just get the bus?'

'Absolutely not,' she said. We've already waited hours for that bloody Doorman. We'll probably end up waiting another hour for the bus. I'm not doing it. No way.'

'Alright.' I said, now resolute that I must learn to drive. If I could then we'd have no use for Doorman and could happily turf him out with no recourse whatsoever.

'What about the handbrake?' said Sheena. 'Isn't that supposed to do something?'

I fumbled around and my hand rested on a lever. 'Is this it?'

'Give it a go,' she said. 'I think you press that little button on the end to make it work.'

I depressed the button and yanked the handbrake, readying myself for my maiden trip.

'That's it!' she said. 'Now hit the accelerator and it should move. Piece of piss.'

I did as she said and the car lurched forward, scraping against the gates of the bin store.

'You did it!' she said. 'Now turn it around and get us out of this shithole.'

Quite miraculously I maneuvered the car out of the turnout and back towards Plugwood Broadway. 'What do I do now?' I said, gazing at the oncoming traffic. 'Just drive into it?'

'Of course,' she said, notably less ebullient than before. 'Although -'

We paused, realising we could quite easily kill ourselves. 'Maybe we should wait until its quieter.'

We shunted back and forth down Ratmouth Street as I attempted to grasp the capabilities of a motor car. It seemed the gears and mirrors were vital but the rest - wipers, headlights, etc. - were superfluous gizmos, unimportant to the business of driving.

After twenty minutes Sheena proclaimed me a better driver than Doorman had ever been, urging me to drive home at the highest possible speeds. 'You're ready.' she said, as assuredly as a spiritual figurehead. 'Let's go.'

Tremulously I joined the traffic and shunted the car along as best I could, intermittently panicking when the engine gnawed at me. At such moments I stamped on the clutch (a trick we'd learnt from a concerned passerby) and wiggled the gearknob in all directions to mitigate the clanking. We crawled along, dodging furious motorists and terrified pedestrians, until we reached the dock road and our building blossomed into view.

'You made it!' said Sheena. 'See? It's easy!'

Despite several brushes with death (none of which were my fault) we'd made it home unscathed. She was right: it *was* easy. Why did people even bother with driving lessons?

'Bit more practice and you could enter a grand prix.' she said.

Maybe I *could* enter a grand prix, I thought, resolving to get the application forms tomorrow.

'Where shall I park?' I said.

'Oh, anywhere,' she said. 'It doesn't matter. I need a drink.'

I left the car by a lamp post and exited, thrilled to have learnt a new life skill. We arrived in the apartment and poured four Warpeckers.

'Do you know what this means?' said Sheena, purposefully jingling the car keys. 'No more buses! No more Doorman!'

I nodded, flinging down my drink and immediately wiring into the next.

'We can drive ourselves now. Mobility at last!' She was practically dancing with excitement, skittering about the room like a ratting terrier.

'Although,' I interjected. 'It *is* Doorman's car. He might want it back.'

'Oh, don't worry about that,' she said. 'We'll call it a downpayment for all the trouble he's caused. Making us wait in the cold, tacking posters up on his walls, that sort of thing.'

'Good thinking,' I said. 'If he argues we'll just evict him.'

'Exactly,' she said. 'Fair's fair.'

An hour later we arrived at the thorny issue of legal representation. I'd suggested legal aid but Sheena quickly dismissed the idea.

'No way,' she said. 'They'd want their money back after we win back our damages. It's a pity defence.'

'Couldn't we just pay for a lawyer?' I said.

She choked on her cig. 'Have you *seen* what they charge?' she said, wheezing out a cloud of Thrushman's smoke. 'Hilary Bell stole four hundred pounds an hour from us. An *hour*. That's money we could've spent on shearling jackets or manuka honey.'

I winced at the figures. I knew from my experience with estate agents that career liars earned a fortune but four hundred pounds an hour was madness.

'Why don't we just represent ourselves?' she said, fabulously unschooled in all facets of law practice. 'I mean, it looks easy, right? Just lie, over and over again. How hard can that be?'

I was immediately convinced, daydreaming of dowdy jurors cowering at my foreboding legal pluck. Once in the courtroom I'd lash them with spittle and demand they send Ed to prison with minimum inmate privileges. I'd insist his visiting hours were nixed and that he be assigned only the most violent and dangerous of cellmates.

'What do you think?' she said, emptying tobacco into her mouth.

'I'm in,' I said. 'Let's destroy him.'

CHAPTER 21

We'd decided to investigate Doorman's specious claims about the changing of the locks. He was clearly lying, but to what end? Would he be waiting for us with the shock prod? We sat in the car park, huffing cigs as I reacquainted myself with the particulars of driving.

'I'm sure this is more complicated than it needs to be,' I said. 'Why are there so many gears?'

'Probably to do with the engine.' said Sheena, barely paying attention. She'd wedged a cig into her asthma inhaler and was working out how to inhale both simultaneously. 'They should start selling Salbutamol cigarettes,' she said. 'Like menthols but for asthmatics. They'd make a fortune.'

'That's a great idea.' I said, not quite listening. I turned the key and the car shuddered to life.

'Do you remember what you're doing?' she said, strapping herself in.

'I think so,' I said. 'Although I can't guarantee I'll hit many cyclists. I'm still learning.'

'Don't worry,' she said. 'I'll throw rocks at them from the window.'

I geed myself up with a brandy miniature and felt my confidence bloom like a ripe jackfruit. 'I'm sure I'll be fine.' I said, buoyed with a tentative optimism.

'Of course you will,' she said, huffing on the inhaler. 'You're a great driver. Now let's get moving.'

We rumbled up the dock road, intermittently crashing into bollards and shipping containers.

'Don't worry about that,' she said. 'This car's on its last legs anyway. Won't be long till we sell it for scrap.'

We drove through Crumbford and I felt my confidence growing. I'd hit a cyclist and was eager to hit more, though I was too inexperienced to ram them with any degree of panache.

'You'll get the hang of it,' said Sheena, hurling a bottle at a binman. 'Remember how long it took you to hit Doorman with a soup tin?'

I nodded, reminding myself that life's greatest triumphs were achieved only with persistence and hard work. It was naive to think I'd master the finer points of driving in a matter of days; I'd need at least a week of practice before reaching a respectable hit rate. We swerved in and out of traffic lanes, breezily cursing any motorist who dared honk us. One disgruntled roaduser, miffed after we'd sheared off his wing mirror at a traffic light, screamed that he'd call the police, a tirade we dismissed with hearty, mocking laughter.

'He probably just needs a shag.' said Sheena.

With a detached bumper and two shattered headlights we arrived at the Plugwood flats, jumpy but exhilarated. Behind the wheel I'd alternated between nonchalant recklessness and terrifying anxiety, weaving between vehicles like a maze runner.

'What's the point of even taking a driving test?' said Sheena. 'When you can learn it all in a couple of days?'

'I don't know,' I said, still shaking. 'Maybe the instructors get handjobs.'

'Sounds about right,' she said. 'Everybody's out for a handjob these days.'

We approached the building and gazed up at its grubby frontage. Hearteningly, it looked unchanged: the garden was still littered with every kind of waste imaginable, while overstuffed binbags spilled their innards across the front path.

'Everything looks in order,' she said. 'We should probably put the rent up again. This place is like a bloody country club.'

I agreed, noting that the scorched grass patches were probably the result of barbecued lobsters.

'They've clearly got money to burn,' she said. 'And we can't afford not to keep up with inflation rates.'

I was sure she was right, yet lacked the financial wherewithal to confirm or deny her claim with any degree of competency. We approached the front door and tried the lock. The key wouldn't fit so I thrust and shoved it, trying valiantly to align the teeth.

'Maybe it's upside down.' she said.

I upturned the key and tried it again, still without joy. 'It's not working.' I said.

'Let me try,' she said, taking the key. 'I used to rob milk depots as a child.' She tussled with the lock and quickly lost her temper. 'What the hell's going on? Why can't we get in? It's *our* building!'

'I think Doorman was right,' I said. 'They have changed the locks.'

Her face grew currant-red as she continued wrestling with the key. 'This is ridiculous. We should call plod.'

'I don't think plod will help us,' I said. 'Let's see if anyone's in.'

'Open the door!' she shrieked, hammering at it with thunderous fists. No reply.

'Perhaps they're on holiday.' I said, hilariously unhelpful.

'All of them?' she barked. 'At the same time? No way. Something's not right here. We need to find out what's going on.'

We'd been so fraught we'd not noticed a van purr up to the curb behind us.

'Step away from the door please madam.' came a voice.

We turned, aghast. What now? Two men had exited the vehicle and were approaching us. They were notably nondescript, dressed like timeless nobodies in button shirts and khaki trousers more commonly spotted on churchgoers.

'Who are you?' said Sheena. 'Get away from me.'

'Come away from the property please madam. You're trespassing and you need to leave now.'

'No way!' she roared. 'This is *our* property and we need to get inside.'

'No you don't, madam,' he said, handing her a heft of documents. 'Check the paperwork'

'What do you mean?' I said. 'We bought it outright.'

'I'm sorry sir, there's nothing I can do. Now please leave or we'll be forced to remove you.'

We were jostled away and advised never to come back. The two enforcers stood guard outside the building until we rattled off in Doorman's shitheap, openly tearful with anger. We parked down a sidestreet and Sheena screamed so loudly I feared I'd develop tinnitus.

'What does the paperwork say?' I said.

She couldn't speak as she was hyperventilating with rage. She was pale and sweating and hair coiled from her head like tangled wire. She yanked open the car door and vomited furiously onto the street. I retrieved the documents and leafed through them, certain I'd be unable to comprehend a single word. I wondered how exactly belching, workaday jurors - those without access to premium law consultancies - were expected to understand such jargon, let alone formulate cogent responses. Thankfully Sheena was both unskilled and workshy, leaving her plenty of time to immerse herself in the minutiae of property regulation.

She raised her head and wiped sick on the car's upholstery. 'They've fucked us,' she said. 'They've fucking fucked us.' She explained that our agreement with the juror had been little more than a handshake, inadmissible as proof of sale.

'What about our money?' I said, naively convinced we'd easily recoup the cash we'd sunk into the flats.

She thrust a page at me, her hand shuddering violently. 'We never paid for them.'

'What?' I said. 'But we did. We paid half price.'

'Read it.'

The document outlined how we'd not paid a penny for the properties, but instead made a generous donation to a mysterious offshore development firm. Additionally there were no contracts, deeds or transactions linking us to the building, nor had we taken out landlords' insurance or contacted the land registry.

'This can't be right,' I said, gophing like a moron. 'The juror said we owned the flats.'

'Turns out we owned nothing,' she said, reading and re-reading the document. 'We were just caretakers.'

'So how do we get our money back?' I said, still disbelieving of the situation. Would we really have to revert back to owning a mere *two* properties? 'Should we call Hilary Bell?'

'Hilary Bell's not our lawyer anymore,' she said, lighting two cigs. 'He wants nothing to do with us.'

'What about Stu? Can he help?'

'He's an estate agent,' she said. 'He only works for the devil.'

We drove home and found a letter wedged under the door. I opened it and was immediately relieved to see the initials of Hilary Bell's law practice. Presumably he'd had a rethink and decided we were honourable clients with whom he'd cultivated a lucrative working relationship. Reading down the page my relief bristled into panic.

'What does it say?' said Sheena, gnawing on a noodle nest.

'It's a summons,' I said. 'Ed's taking us to court.'

'Oh we know that already,' she said. 'We're going to

represent ourselves. Piece of piss'

'I don't think we're going to win,' I said, handing her the letter. 'Hilary Bell's taken him on as a client.'

Her face ballooned like a cooked sausage. 'Hilary Bell's representing Ed? How did that happen? What are we going to do?'

I didn't answer. I was reading the second page of the letter. 'Oh my god.' I said, stunned.

'What?' she said, snatching it from me. 'What else?' Her gaze darkened as she read what I'd just read. Her eyes grew red as the ramifications dawned on her. 'No,' she stammered. 'No, no, no. This can't be happening.'

I buried my head in a cushion as she began a rampage that lasted several hours: a frenzied, tornado-like barnstorm during which I feared for every stick of furniture we owned. The brushed steel knife block, that which I'd coveted so passionately, was ripped from the wall and hurled out of the window, striking the neighbours' dog with a blow the euthanizing vet later called 'tragically improbable'. She tore stuffing from pillows and threw chairs at windows, yanked wires from appliances and smashed over a hundred kitchen tiles.

The document (now torn to shreds) that'd so infuriated Sheena was an itemised list of the damages being sought by Ed. Taking into consideration lost earnings, therapy fees, physical and psychological trauma, the total amounted to £695,000.00, coincidentally the exact resale value of our apartment.

Sheena was slumped against the wall, whimpering and covered in blood. 'What are we going to do?' she said. 'We're screwed. We'll have to sell this place.'

I had no answer. Our only option was to beat Hilary Bell in court, a laughably unlikely scenario given his formidable legal clout. He'd crush us like cat biscuits and we both knew it.

'I can't lose my home,' she said. 'I can't go back to renting.'

'We've still got Ed's property,' I said. 'We could live there.'

'It's been registered as uninhabitable,' she said. 'No one can live there legally. Plus, it's a shithole.'

'We could give it a lick of paint, make it nice.' I said, convincing no one. (Little did we know it'd already been overrun by dampwood termites.)

She snorted and rose from the floor. She had cuts up and down her arms and walked with a limp, an aftereffect of stamping the coffee table to pieces. 'When's the trial?' she said, dribbling drain cleaner onto her wounds.

I scrabbled about for the ripped letter and confirmed we were due in court in two weeks.

'That's it then,' she said. 'Two weeks. That's all we've got left. Better make the most of it.'

More so than ever before, we'd tussled with implacable forces and had, somewhat predictably, been outmanoeuvred. It was the first time during our reign that I'd seen her genuinely defeated. Would she kill herself? Quite possibly. Prior to our acquisition of property she'd been suicidally depressed, often leaving the gas on in an attempt to die in her sleep, but was ultimately saved by the inextinguishable hope that one day she'd be able to give up work and own a flat. Seeing her dreams made manifest had been the happiest moment of her life, she'd told me, and the assemblage of a property portfolio had provided both purpose and direction. To have it all snatched away was surely the cruellest outcome imaginable, and would doubtlessly send her right back to huffing carbon monoxide in an unventilated bedsit.

'We'll have nothing,' she said, mindlessly plastering electrical tape onto her arm. 'Nothing.'

I tried mustering some words of comfort but drew a blank. I simply couldn't conceive of a life encumbered by financial struggle or housing poverty. 'We could sell the car.' I said, wondering if rag and bone men still existed. 'That might help.'

'Worthless,' she said. 'Wouldn't cover our drink budget for a week.'

'So -' I paused, still vaguely uncomprehending. 'How are we going to survive?'

She pursed her lips and tried not to cry. 'I don't think we are.'

CHAPTER 22

The next two weeks passed miserably. We should've been using the time to prepare our defence, contact witnesses, bribe jurors, etc., but were unable to summon even a kilojoule of energy. Despite everything we'd suffered, things never seemed bleaker. Like mortgage applicants we trudged through the days, despondent and glumly accepting of our predestined failure.

We kept drinking, but with little enjoyment. Ordinarily I'd skull twelve tins of *Murgs* during depressive periods, a coping strategy guaranteed to stimulate brain activity and increase dopamine production, yet it now cast over me a glutinous and immovable despair. Most days I lay in bed, sweating butter over my bedsheets and smoking Thrushman's until my uvula throbbed, wondering how on earth we'd defeat Hilary Bell in court.

Sheena was faring even worse. She'd resolved not to clean the apartment after her rampage, reasoning that'd be a job for the creditors who'd eventually snatch our home from us. This meant the floors remained carpeted in glass and our feet were routinely chewed to pieces as we shuffled to the kitchen to gobble potted pig.

Her mental health had also taken a terrifying nosedive. She barely got out of bed, instead spending her days pulling out her eyelashes and making panicked calls to crisis centres. She drank constantly, amassing bottles and gagging on asthma cigarettes until I thought she might combust. Her face had turned a mustard shade of grey and her teeth periodically fell out, littering the carpet like sweetcorn kernels. Her breath, ordinarily a pungent blend of alcohol and tar, was now infused with the vomitous tang of halitosis, gifting her the questionable ability to kill airborne flies with a single exhalation.

Neither of us bothered changing our clothes, and after a week I noticed tiny worm slugs threading glistening trails among the folds of my cable knit. I was so fatigued I couldn't muster the energy to wipe them away, instead staring, hypnotised, at their slow and slimy labours. Even more worrying was Sheena's dressing gown, a thinning rag so moist with sweat that little weed tufts had sprouted from the collar and armpits.

It was a Tuesday, and we were lying on the sofas in a cloud of brown smoke, eating hen necks and tossing painkillers into our mouths like peanuts.

'When's the court case?' said Sheena, her voice shredded beyond surgery.

'I don't know,' I said. 'Two weeks?'

She wedged a Thrushman's into her inhaler and took a noxious huff. 'Are you sure?' she said. 'Isn't it sooner than that?'

I rose and combed through the post that'd collected beneath the letterbox. Among the letters was a reminder from the court. I tore it open. 'It's tomorrow.' I said, utterly unfazed. I'd resigned myself to the fact that we'd lose our home and felt a tremulous thrill at having no backup plan whatsoever. I'd assumed Sheena would return to her job at the cafe while I'd pick up freelance work as a diamond cutter or truffle huntsman, quickly recouping the cash we'd need to buy back our treasured apartment.

'Should we start preparing our defence? I said, calmly binning the letter.

'Yeah, probably,' said Sheena. 'What do we need for

182

that?'

'I don't know,' I said. 'Pens?'

'Yes, pens,' she said. 'Where's a pen?'

We found a betting pen in Doorman's car and sketched out a plan on a toilet roll. We agreed to lie about the gas safety certificate, claiming the postman had fallen ill and not delivered our confirmation letter.

'Postmen get ill all the time,' she said. 'Cat diseases.'

'Very true.' I said.

We also decided to smear Ed's character, claiming he was a predator who administered illegal blood facials to dementia patients.

'I'd believe it,' I said, now deeply immersed in our fantasy. 'It's exactly the type of thing he'd do.'

'He's a monster.' she said, fully in agreement.

We conjured further lies; mostly harmless tattle about his history of indecent exposure, baby kidnapping and livestock torture, reasoning the more accusations we hurled around the higher the probability of the jury questioning his credibility.

'They'll believe anything,' said Sheena, picking gristle from her gums. 'They're just members of the public, after all. Scum, basically.'

'We could tell them anything,' I laughed. 'They'll be too busy eating chips to make an informed decision.'

~

The next morning we awoke and discarded Hilary Bell's spineless advice about court protocol. We didn't bother dressing for the occasion, convinced we'd lose everything and unconcerned with arbitrary fashion standards. Instead we remained in our pyjamas and stuffed our pockets with cigs and miniatures, vital fuel for our forthcoming humiliation.

'Let's get this over with,' said Sheena, tearing at her fingernails and swinging her dressing gown cord like a hangman's noose.

We hesitated before leaving the apartment, recognising with some sadness that this was effectively the end of the life we'd crafted for ourselves. I cursed myself for my complacency in the face of such ease. With our purchase of the apartment I'd assumed my life as a solvent homeowner had been an unimpeachable certainty; that any sorrow befalling us would remain firmly outside the confines of our homestead, shut out from the grandiloquence of our most cherished asset. Never had I imagined it'd be taken from us, rendering us not only homeless, but also necessitating the need for gainful employment, surely the grisliest horror it was possible to inflict. 'Should we say goodbye?' I said, suddenly overwhelmed with sentiment.

'I was thinking that,' said Sheena. 'Maybe we should.'

Unsure what this entailed, we drifted back inside and gravitated towards our favourite spots. Sheena edged towards the balcony, while I bumbled into the kitchen to caress my espresso machine. Wistfully tracing its curvature with a finger, I heard a faint *clink, clink, clink* from Sheena's direction. I emerged onto the balcony and found her with a boxful of possessions (bottles, bath towels, cutlery) that she was successively hurling over the edge.

'What are you doing?' I said, wondering how I'd dry my knackers without the requisite stockpile of towels.

'I don't know,' she said. 'I just want to get rid of everything.'

I took a groove weeder from the box and tossed it. There was no Doorman to retrieve it, nor any neighbours to complain. The morning was silent, broken only by the neutered clatter of cortado mugs crashing on tarmac. The contents of the box dwindled as the debris field widened, forming a fragmented blast radius.

'Shall we get more?' I said, now with an insatiable thirst for recklessness.

'Absolutely.' she said.

We proceeded to hurl our possessions off the balcony, howling deliriously as they thudded and tinkled on the ground below.

'That's everything,' I said, surveying the wreckage. 'We're done.'

The apartment stood behind us, desecrated and bare.

'Let's go.' said Sheena.

I skulled a gin livener and started the car. I found the alcohol caused a welcome increase in confidence when driving, loosening my inhibitions and enabling me to take risks that spirited us to our destination in enviable time. Often I'd swerve across lanes of traffic without checking my mirrors, honking indiscriminately and flashing my lights like a wedding DJ. Other roadusers, while angry, seemed respectful of my methods, dropping back and allowing me adequate room to manoeuvre. It went some way to reframing my opinion of motorists not only as jack-wielding meatheads, as it became clear they were also cowards, terrified of a fortuitous road accident. Surely a shattered sternum warranted at least a month off work?

Despite my motoring prowess I only managed to hit three cyclists, ramming them with the blasé assuredness of an intoxicated premiership footballer.

'Did you see that last one go down?' whooped Sheena, laughing and clapping. 'Right into a tree!'

The damage to the tree was unfortunate but unavoidable: if I'd hesitated a second longer he would've got away. Solemnly I vowed to plant a sapling at the earliest opportunity.

We were met outside court by a flurry of journalists swarming around the car, hungry for salacious content and upskirt genital images. They thumped the windows and photographed the bloodied bonnet, later claiming we sacrificed animals to appease the gods of profit (if only!). I jerked the car forward and managed to mow down two such pests, one of whom spent the rest of his life in a leg brace. They quickly scattered, trampling their fallen comrades and haranguing us as we ascended the steps, eager to extract pull-quotes and incriminating snippets of conversation. We remained silent, flicking lit cigs into the throng in the hope one of them might lose an eye. Once again we arrived in the courthouse lobby, this time without legal counsel and wobbly from drink.

'Is there a bar in here?' said Sheena, sneering dismissively at a coffee machine.

'I don't think so,' I said, tossing her a miniature. 'Thank god we brought our own.'

We slouched on a bench outside the courtroom and were told several times to stop smoking, an order we ignored until threatened with ejection from the building. Finally we were called in and took our seats as before. Sheena elbowed me and pointed across the room. For the first time since the gas explosion I saw Ed. His face was craggy and ridged and his skin looked like it'd been vacuum-sealed in a polythene bag. His top lip had been sheared off and he wore a patch over one eye.

'He looks fine,' said Sheena. 'Big fuss over nothing.'

I nodded, squinting to make out the extent of Ed's injuries. His nose was pocked with stitches and his jaw seemed oddly fattened and amorphous, like it'd been pulped together with papier mache. Propped beside him were two walking sticks, presumably an affectation to elicit sympathy from the judge.

We took our seats and I could hear the hateful yammering of the grasping press representatives. Surveying their avaricious faces I wondered how this could possibly be in the public interest. Surely no one wanted to hear more ungrateful grousing from the renting classes?

We were instructed to rise before the honourable Lord Justice Wretchley, as if he were a vengeful Edwardian king. He strode in and took his seat before us. For a second I caught his eye and gleaned a momentary sadness. Would he take pity on us?

Hilary Bell, seated beside Ed, quickly snapped to

action, outlining the charges and positing the outrageous notion that we were criminals. He labelled us slum landlords whose greed, neglect and incompetence had endangered the life of an innocent young man, hospitalising and ultimately costing him the use of his legs.

'That's rubbish, for a start,' whispered Sheena in my ear. 'I saw him stroll in here with those walking sticks.'

Wretchley hushed her with an inveterate weariness. Hilary Bell continued, somehow managing to convince even me, that we were parasites profiting handsomely from the common need for shelter. He detailed the chest freezer used to store contaminated livers, the black slime that coated every wall, and the respiratory disease for which Ed was being treated, apparently so resistant to treatment that he'd require an oxygen tank within three years.

'Sounds like a laugh,' said Sheena. 'He could turn it into a jet pack.'

I nodded in agreement. He worked with computers so programming a jet propulsion flight system would no doubt be a doddle. 'It'd also cut his travel costs significantly.' I said. 'Sounds like he's getting a good deal.'

Hilary Bell exposited further: the mould was so rampant it'd birthed a new, as-yet-unclassified strain of virus comparable only to lepromatous leprosy. Ed, predictably, had been infected, and was under periodic observation at the Pratford Disease Research Centre, a famously unsanitary prison complex suspected of harbouring physicians from fallen dictatorships. Supposedly this, too, was our fault.

'Lucky bastard,' said Sheena. 'I'd love a stay in a comfy hospital.'

'Me too,' I said. 'Think of all the complimentary grapes.'

'Some people are never satisfied.' she said, shooting a glance at Ed's lesioned face. 'We give him a beautiful flat and he throws it back in our faces.'

Wretchley slammed his gavel and told us to be quiet.

Having slandered us into the ground, Hilary Bell concluded his tirade with the assertion that we should be banned from ever renting property, that we should pay over six hundred thousand pounds in damages, and that we should be imprisoned for a minimum of five years.

'That's crazy!' roared Sheena, attracting judgemental stares. The jury, meanwhile, sat like cattle, many of them grateful simply for the time off work, and stared dumbly as she protested our innocence. Did they even know where they were? They resembled a pond full of carp, opening and closing their mouths as they grappled with the concepts of law, some blowing bubbles, others distracted by their own shoelaces.

We were then requested to give an opening statement of our own. We'd agreed, given Sheena's incorrigible temper, that I would do this, hopefully providing some semblance of a coherent argument. I approached the front of the court and could feel the sweat threading down my face, moistening my skin like a neglected ham loin.

'Hello,' I said, gasping for an espresso. 'My business partner and I believe the services we provided to our tenant were perfectly reasonable.' I saw Hilary Bell wince. 'When we rented him the property it was pristine.' I said, grasping to remember the list of lies we'd concocted. 'It had lovely carpets, chandeliers, and a beautiful tall tub dishwasher. When we heard about the explosion we visited the property and were shocked by what he'd done to the place. It was disgusting.' Did that sound convincing?

I continued my erudite ramble for several long minutes, detailing the palatial splendour blighted by Ed's tenancy. In an effort to help our cause I gesticulated wildly at the jurors, who were no doubt daydreaming about nursery rhymes and football, but failed to elicit even a speck of sympathy.

Mercifully putting me out of my misery, Wretchley then requested Hilary Bell call the first of his witnesses, namely the old woman who lived on the top floor of the flats. She was a crumbly old goblin, speckled with liverspots and dressed like an eccentric colonialist (tattered fedora, tan smock) whose hands I imagined were stained with the blood of the oppressed. We assumed she'd been paid to lie in court, presumably remunerated with bobby pins or discounted heating tariffs, because she spun fallacious yarns about our abandonment of our responsibilities, our mistreatment of tenants, our chronic alcoholism, etc., all fabricated tosh that caused us involuntary snorts of incredulity. 'Clearly demented,' said Sheena. 'Silly old bat.'

The next witness was then called. Encouragingly it was the student I'd previously met at the flats; she who'd seemed, quite extraordinarily, to be of sound mind. Her arm rested in a sling and she seemed notably uncomfortable, answering monosyllabically to Hilary Bell's devious lines of questioning. I squinted as she spoke, noticing red marks studding her cheek and neck. Had they tried to eat her?

Finally Hilary Bell called Roy Foggins to the witness box; a name I'd completely forgotten until Doorman hobbled up before us. It was the first time we'd seen him since he'd disappeared and he looked worse than ever. He wore a cervical collar around his neck and had two black eyes, while his cheeks were bloated with blue and purple bruises. 'Serves him right.' said Sheena.

He proceeded to smear our characters with a slew of indefensible lies, claiming we'd gotten him sacked, stolen his car, commandeered his bed and thrown his duvet out of the window.

'That's bullshit!' roared Sheena, hurling a pen at him. Wretchley looked down at us, his expression suggesting we were now beyond help.

We had no witnesses to call, so instead I made a borderline incomprehensible closing statement. I stuttered something about our being tricked into caretaking the flats, our looming insolvency, our expulsion from the Ten Hours, but it all came across as the stunted mutterings of a halfwit.

The jury then muddled out to decide our fates, a terrifying thought given their collective stupidity, while we waited like fairground ducks.

'Do you think we'll get off?' said Sheena, her hands trembling from fear and alcoholism.

'I'm sure we will.' I said, gently lying through my teeth.

They were back out in ten minutes, and delivered a Guilty verdict without a second thought. I primed myself for an outburst but Sheena remained silent, motionlessly staring at her feet. Had she fainted? 'Are you okay?' I said.

'We're done,' she said. 'That's it. Ruined.'

We sat, utterly defeated and unable to speak, and awaited Wretchley's return.

'Ruined.' she muttered again.

Was this it? The end of our glorious reign? I feared what a return to work might do for her health. From even a basic physiological perspective, the withdrawal from even a minor break with drinking could completely destroy her, so it was imperative she found employment that enabled at least a baseline level of alcoholism. Perhaps something in the advertising industry?

The court fell silent as Wretchley reappeared, ready to deliver our sentence. He looked on us with a strange, paternal disappointment, much like Dad when he caught me with the stolen leper's bell. The words echoed from his mouth in slow motion, tightening around us like gastric bands: '...hereby ordered to pay the sum of six hundred and ninety-five thousand pounds...' I choked. I felt Sheena's hand on my forearm. '...a lifetime ban from renting property...' My throat billowed with vomit. '...two thousand hours of community service...suspended prison sentence...' His gavel slammed down.

Sheena looked at me. 'Ruined.' she said.

The room immediately blustered to life: journalists swooped from the rafters while jurors picked their noses and gabbed about their favourite shapes. We were escorted from the room by uniformed men who shoved us out to the corridor, muttering something about peoples' justice.

'Get off me!' roared Sheena, swiping at them with her stubby nails. 'We've done nothing wrong!'

Once outside we were mobbed by newspeople. They barked at us in an effort to elicit saleable copy but we were too dizzied to respond with any degree of coherence. Among the crowd were the two ground floor tenants with whom we'd previously tussled, laughing and whooping and spitting peanuts in our faces.

'What'll you do now?' yelled a journalist, waving a recorder in our faces.

'Is this the end of your reign of terror?' bawled another, implying we'd somehow behaved unreasonably.

We jostled through the cluster. Flailing arms and hands surrounded us as we stumbled forward, elbowing in the face anyone standing in our way. 'Out of the way, scum!' I said, knocking people over on our approach to the car. We fell inside, kicking and thrashing as the rapacious scribes tried furiously to extract content from our innocent mouths.

'Go!' said Sheena, cramming her mouth with cigs. I hit two journalists as we pulled off, disabling them with a satisfying, biscuity crunch. We sped off, leaving the frenzied mass to hunt elsewhere for lies.

We headed home but press vehicles were backed up the dock road, staking out our building.

'Down here,' said Sheena, yanking a hard left on the steering wheel. 'Hurry up.'

She guided us between two rows of shipping containers and into a small clearing. We were surrounded by huge, corrugated iron crates, imposingly stacked in columns of three. 'What's this?' I said, stopping the car.

'Doorman lives here.' she said, heaving open a rusty container door. 'He moved in after they changed the locks at the flats. Apparently he used it as a break room when he worked in our building.'

Inside was heartbreakingly squalid; as dank and musty

as Grandma's back pantry. It smelt like overstewed vegetables and the container ceiling was brown with rust. Socks and underpants hung limply from wall-mounted haulage chains and bats slept peacefully in the corners. Judging by the lumpen human imprint it seemed he'd been sleeping on a couple of oat sacks, presumably donated by the Grotley miners' union relief effort. I also recognised the sackcloth I'd lent him during his stay in our apartment, now threadbare and scrabbled to ribbons by vermin. 'Did he pinch that?' I said, too disheartened to summon the requisite outrage.

'Probably.' said Sheena, crumpling into a heap. 'Who even cares?'

It was then I knew she was beaten. Following her lead, I dropped to the floor and slept for what seemed like yonks.

We awoke to clanging feet and hectoring voices. 'Come on, let's go.' they honked. 'Time to get up.'

'What's happening?' I said, still cobwebbed from my snooze. 'Is it breakfast time? Could we have some croissants?'

'And Beaujolais.' croaked Sheena, still half asleep.

We were dragged to our feet by the two security men who'd previously barred us from entering the flats. They wore their customary civvies; pale polyester and overstarched denim that wouldn't have looked out of place on a local neighbourhood moron. Despite their calamitous appearance they were prenaturally strong, levering us to our feet like featherweight bird skeletons. They hauled us outside and we squawked as our retinas were blasted with daylight. Had we slept all night?

Before us stood Doorman, his brow furrowed and his skin weathered by freezing outdoor protests.

'Doorman,' I said. 'Get these tossers off us.'

He shook his head and wouldn't look us in the eye. 'Sorry,' he said. 'There's nothing I can do.' I noticed blueish bruising around his neck.

192

'Come on, off with you,' said the security men. 'This isn't your property. We know what you're like. Can't risk you trying to rent it out.'

'Fine, fine,' I said. 'We just fell asleep. We didn't even want to stay here.'

'Exactly,' said Sheena. 'We wouldn't stay in this shithole if you paid us.'

'Let's go,' I said, fumbling for the car keys. 'It's only a short drive home.'

'Sorry,' said Doorman, the keys jingling in his hand. 'That's my car.'

'Piss off Doorman,' said Sheena. 'Give us back the car.'

He stared at us, silent, cowed, ashamed. There was nothing we could do.

CHAPTER 23

We tramped up the dock road, aching and dirty, to the apartment building, where a solitary journalist lay, snoring and half-drunk, on the lobby steps. He jolted slobbishly upon hearing us, but slipped back into his stupor upon realising the rest of the newspeople had gone.

'Where are they all?' said Sheena. 'I thought we were front page news?'

They'd left a field of debris outside the building: cigs, beer cans, wires, paper, matches, all trampled into the surrounding grass verge.

We rode the lift to our apartment and approached the door. Tacked to it was a repossession notice informing us the place was now in the hands of creditors who'd auction it off at the earliest opportunity. There was a padlock to ensure we were kept out, and our remaining possessions were stuffed in boxes in the hallway.

'What do we do now?' said Sheena. 'Kill ourselves?'

Despite seeming like the only viable option, I suggested we visit Stu, as he'd surely greet us with warmth and cava. 'We've banked plenty of goodwill with him,' I said. 'He'll probably rent us a flat for free. As a thank you for all our hard work.'

'Great idea,' said Sheena. 'We earned him two big commissions, after all.'

Heartbreakingly, we had to ride the *bus* to Stu's office, a nightmarish ordeal that saw us packed like dog meat amid a surplus of feckless human slurry. It felt like we'd hitched a ride in a populist hate wagon, as leathery, racist divorcees yakked about the halcyon days of the 70s and bemoaned multiculturalism like Gestapo enforcers. Eavesdropping on one such conversation I discerned they were angry at a news story in which an immigrant had been prescribed paracetamol by a British doctor, apparently an affront to the memory of fallen servicemen. ('It ain't right!' they crowed.)

We arrived at the estate agents' office and loitered in the waiting area. 'Stu!' we called. 'We need a flat!'

He appeared from a back room with his shirtsleeves rolled up, exposing formidable cephalic veins. Had he been gutting a tenant? 'Oh hey guys.' he said, seemingly exhausted by the sight of us. 'What's up? I'm a bit busy right now.'

'We need a flat,' said Sheena. 'And two bottles of cava.'

He winced, squeezing his neck with a bulbous forearm. 'Listen guys,' he said. 'I don't think that's going to be so easy right now.'

'Why?' I said. 'Is it because of the market?' (I'd heard Sheena mention the market during such negotiations.)

'Not really,' he said, notably evasive. 'It's a little bit more complicated than that.'

'Well, let's sit down and talk about it,' said Sheena. 'You get the cava and we'll wait in the back room.'

'Um, no, I can't do that either I'm afraid.' he said.

'Why not?' she said. 'We got you two commissions. All we're asking for is a couple of bottles of cava. You've probably got loads of it in your fridge.'

He looked around the empty office. 'Okay, quickly,' he said, locking the front door. 'Come with me.'

We followed him to the back room and took our usual seats. Oddly, he sat down with us, apparently oblivious to our appetent thirst. 'Look guys,' he said. 'It's over. I can't help you anymore.'

'We don't want your help, Stu,' said Sheena. 'All we want is two bottles of cava and a lovely flat to live in. You're an estate agent, aren't you? Sort it out.'

'I can't give you any cava,' he said, his triceps tensed. 'And no more special treatment. If you want a flat you're going to have to pay for one.'

'That's crazy,' I said. 'Just give us a flat. There are loads of them in your window.'

'There's another problem.' he said, his forehead now spotting perspiration. 'There's been some new legislation passed. Around renting.'

'What do you mean?' said Sheena. 'What legislation?'

Stu outlined the new laws that'd quietly been passed over the last couple of weeks. With horror we recognised what he described: it was the bill we'd dreamt up with the health secretary, spangled on parliamentary cocaine, in the Ten Hours Club. He detailed the new regulations: non-refundable deposits, fee increases, erosion of tenants' rights, all hilarious until we realised the implications.

'You don't mean -' I said, dumbstruck.

'This wouldn't apply to *us*, surely?' said Sheena. 'We're property owners, not scummy rental tenants. We're landlords.'

Stu gurned like a cage fighter. 'Sorry guys,' he said. 'There's nothing I can do.'

We left the office trembling. Sheena spotted a van speeding towards us and stepped out in front of it, prompting me to yank her back onto the pavement. The van screeched, swerving into a layby and hospitalising a dog walker. 'What are you doing?' I said, quietly envious of her recklessness.

'I just thought I'd get it over with,' she said. 'Quick and painless.'

'I understand,' I said, trying to stall her. 'But don't you want to wait until rush hour? Inconvenience a few commuters?'

She buried her face in her cashmere. 'That'd be nice,' she whispered. 'Make them late for work.'

'How about we buy some whisky?' I said, as warmly as a crack dealer. She nodded and I surreptitiously guided her away from the traffic. She walked beside me, silently staring at the pavement.

'Are you angry?' I said, mildly spooked by her quietude. (When would she start throwing knives at shopkeepers?)

'Of course I am,' she said, following a timorous pause. 'But there's nothing we can do.'

She was right, this wasn't like before. We couldn't simply blackmail MPs and high court judges and expect a fair return; the weight of power was too great. All we could do now was find a way to survive.

We couldn't afford Warpecker, so opted instead for a bottle of Old Mudbin, an undrinkable cooking whisky made famous by an 80s terror cell who used it to make pipebombs.

We shuffled up Plugwood Broadway and retched trying to keep the drink down. I felt layers of my pharynx peeling away as the raw alcohol sheared my throat. Would I still be able to scream?

'Where are we going to sleep tonight?' said Sheena, tears glistening in her eyes.

It was then I realised we had nowhere to go. We'd been shut out of everywhere we'd once called home. 'What about the shipping container?' I said.

'Doorman sleeps there,' she said. 'And he hates us.'

'But he's our servant -' I said, immediately realising my mistake. Without a rotten bedsit to dangle before him, he had no cause to remain in our servitude. He was free of us.

'What about Ed's old flat?'

'Condemned,' said Sheena. 'Plus it'll be sold off to cover our fine.'

We walked on in silence. It'd started to rain; a freezing, spitting coverage, and I was concerned for my lambswool. I'd need somewhere warm to dry it after such a soaking.

'Hey, look where we are.' said Sheena.

Near the end of the street was a man emptying an offal bucket into the gutter. A closer squint identified him as Muggins, proprietor of Muggins Cafe.

'Have we really walked that far?' I said, disoriented by the lashings of Old Mudbin.

'Yep,' said Sheena. 'We're at Plugwood Lock.'

We hurried towards him, thrilled to find somewhere we'd be gifted cow meat and Chardonnay.

'Hey Muggins,' she called. He looked up, his face sticky with rapeseed oil. 'Two cow meat platters.'

'And a bottle of Chardonnay!' I added. (The sugars helped neutralise the meat's sour notes).

'Friends!' he said, admirably delighted to see us. 'Come inside, you're soaked!' He seated us by a radiator and wrapped us in polythene sheeting. 'What happened?' he said. 'You look exhausted.'

'We've been walking for hours,' said Sheena. 'I'm so thirsty.'

Without a word he fetched a bottle of wine and set it down between us. 'Drink this, friends,' he said. 'I'll fetch your cow meat.'

We drank the bottle in thirty seconds, pouring it down our throats with no satiety reflex whatsoever. It tasted flinty, with an acidic afterburn that suggested a cost-saving vinegar dilution.

'I'm still thirsty,' said Sheena, flapping her arms at Muggins. 'More wine!' It seemed her strength was returning. The capillaries on her cheeks were pronounced, spidering her skin like the footprints of a bird. I caressed the radiator, absorbing its heat and feeling my chill subside. Muggins returned with a second bottle and two plates, both heaped with steaming grey scraps. 'Bon appetit.' he said proudly.

We filled our mouths with the dry, gristly turf, chewing with the veracity of people weakened by mild to moderate hunger. My teeth squeaked as I gnawed through the calloused, boiling leather, unaware it'd be the last human meal I'd eat for several days.

As before, the wine was finished almost immediately, although we'd grown sloppy and spilled it on our chins and clothes. The cafe had quietened as the patrons tired of the abuse being hurled their way, filing out with derisory tuts until only the owner remained.

Our plates were strewn with fat pucks and blobby, half-chewed sinews. We reclined like bipedal grubs, belching as we gasped down digestif cigs. It was dark outside and the owner locked the front door, a pointless formality given the worthlessness of his premises. 'Time to head home now, friends,' he said. 'I'm sure you've lots to be getting on with.'

Sheena and I exchanged furtive glances. We were both drunk and desperately tired, our eyes drooping like wet teabags.

'Come now, friends,' he said. 'The cafe's closed.'

Untethered from shame or inhibition we decided to fall squarely on his mercy. 'Have you got a spare room?' said Sheena. 'We need somewhere to stay.'

He smiled almost imperceptibly. 'What happened?' he said, pulling down the shutters. 'Have you got termites?'

'I wish,' she said, looking to me for backup. 'There's a few issues with our building.'

'Yes,' I said, grasping for a plausible lie. 'We've got knotweed.'

'Terrible knotweed,' added Sheena quickly. 'It's attacking the foundations.'

'How *awful*,' said Muggins, taking a seat between us. 'It's such an invasive species.'

'I know,' I said. 'We're waiting for a delivery of plant lice.' What *was* I talking about?

'So you see,' said Sheena, 'we're a bit stuck at the moment. We'd like to stay here please.'

Muggins gurned theatrically. 'I'm sorry friends,' he said. 'I've not got any room right now. I've got a couple of online scammers staying upstairs. Lovely boys.' Had he guessed how desperate we were?

'However -'

I knew exactly what he was going to suggest.

'There's always room *downstairs*.'

We looked at each other, then out at the freezing nighttime. Sleet pelted the street like gunfire and the wind blasted in wet, icy gusts.

'Is there a heater down there?' I said, starting to shiver.

He laughed and shook his head. 'I'm sorry, no,' he said. 'It's not a five-star hotel, you know!'

'What about food?' said Sheena. 'Would we have to eat compost scraps?'

He looked at us, then at our plates, his head cocked in sympathy. 'Well I can't give you *all* my cow meat, can I?' he said. 'There'd be none left for the customers.'

'Yes, I suppose you're right,' I said. 'What about bedding? Do you provide goosedown comforters?'

'I can't promise anything,' he said, retrieving a rusty key from his pocket. 'But there might still be some lino offcuts down there. That's if my wife didn't eat them all.'

'Okay,' said Sheena. 'We'll stay. But if you try to keep us prisoner we'll tear your cafe to pieces.'

His face swelled into a rictus grin. 'Follow me.' he said.

CHAPTER 24

Muggins lead us through the kitchen, past the fat scrapers, the drums of frying oil, the blood-spattered aprons, to the familiar door of the cellar. 'Don't worry about the first night's rent,' he said. 'I know things are tough right now.'

We stopped dead. 'Rent?' I said.

'What are you talking about?' said Sheena.

'You can't stay here for free, friends,' he said, incredulous that we'd dared to think otherwise. 'That's not how the market works.'

'But it's disgusting,' she said. 'It's a horrible little cellar. How can you expect us to pay money for that?'

'You're welcome to find somewhere else,' he said. 'But I've got people queuing up to rent this place. Take it or leave it, friends.'

We agreed to his ludicrous demands, mentally resolving never to pay him a penny. We also knew that soliciting us directly would save him a hefty agency fee, a saving he'd invariably pass on to us.

'Fine,' said Sheena. 'How much?'

'Great.' he said, unpocketing a wad of documents. 'It's four hundred a week, bills not included. Shall we set up a direct debit? We can do it all online.'

'Four hundred a week?' I said. 'But it's damp and horrible. There's mould all over the walls.'

He laughed, with a callousness previously unseen. 'Just a bit of wear and tear,' he said. 'Nothing to worry about.'

Without collateral or room for negotiation, we shook his hand and signed his contract, reasoning Stu would help out with any legal problems encountered forthwith.

'Welcome to your new home!' said Muggins, scraping open the cellar door. 'It's a great little space, plenty of cute little mice running around, great access to local amenities,' he tailed off, having exhausted all the virtues of a freezing basement.

We descended the stairs and our nostrils tickled with the musty reek of damp. It was a crushing, overwhelming stink, one imbued with all the weight of our former destitution.

'Have a great night, friends,' said Muggins. 'See you at feeding time tomorrow.'

Too drunk and exhausted to argue, we slumped to the floor.

'I'm so tired,' said Sheena. 'All I want to do is smoke fifty cigs and sleep forever.'

'Sounds good,' I said, quickly drifting off.

I awoke in agonising pain, shattered after a bone-crunching night on the concrete. I looked over at Sheena, who was somehow still asleep despite the sub-zero temperatures. Her face was charred with ash and her lips were blotched white with burn marks where she'd fallen asleep smoking. Discarded Thrushman's butts littered the floor and her clothes were so pocked with cig burns her cashmere resembled a woollen colander.

The cellar was even filthier than I remembered. Rat droppings peppered the floor, black and clusterful like nigella seeds, while the packing crates had begun to deteriorate, sodden by the omnipresent, sporing mould. The room was lit by a single lightbulb, affixed to an overhead beam, that cast over us a milky yellow glow. There were no windows, nor any elegant uplighting, nor had Muggins provided dressing gowns of any kind. I assumed, as with our previous apartment, that there'd be a welcome hamper awaiting us: an ostentatious bouquet of fermented brisket and premium pig cheese that'd provide valuable arterial insulation due to its saturated fat content.

I bundled up my gnarled old testicles and rose from the floor. I tiptoed over to Sheena, keeping an eye out for rats.

'Sheena,' I hissed. 'Let's go. We can't stay here.' She didn't move. I nudged her gently, knowing how much she hated being woken up. (She'd once ripped a cat's head off after it'd jumped into bed for a snuggle). Still not a twitch. I didn't worry unnecessarily, aware she'd often sleep for eighteen hours at a time, rising only when the screaming alcohol withdrawal shocked her back to life. Interestingly, the attending doctor later mentioned that if I'd woken her up right then, instead of leaving her brain cells to deoxygenate and die, there was a chance I could've saved her life.

Unfortunately for Sheena however, I was shuffling around the cellar as she lay dying, debating whether to eat the compost scraps wilting in the feed bowl. *Not right now*, I thought, my belly still swelled from the cow meat banquet. Still unconscious, she then thrashed and choked, growing godlessly pale as a hypoxic brain injury killed her in her sleep. Blissfully unaware, I regarded all this as perfectly normal, idly kneading my scrotum and daydreaming about moka pots. Would I ever enjoy such kitchenware again?

I came to Sheena's assistance only after a particularly guttural whoop caught my attention. I knelt beside her and tried shaking her awake, unperturbed by her cold blue mouth and inanimate eyelids. 'Let's get you a brandy.' I said, hoping the mention of drink would be enough to ignite her consciousness. No reply. 'Sheena,' I said. 'Can you wake up please? It's horrible down here.' I noticed she wasn't breathing but assumed this was symptomatic of her one lung. I looked closer and noticed her eyes weren't dilating. I checked her pulse and felt nothing. It was then I began to panic: an anxious, manic rush similar to the thrill of dumping a long-term partner. She couldn't be *dead*, could she?

I balked at the thought of funeral arrangements. Would I be required to cart her body back to Wales? I hadn't the means to hire a van, but wondered if I might squeeze her into a packing crate and bribe a lorry driver with amphetamines and prostitution vouchers.

Furthermore, would I be required to attend? The shortlist was sparse. Her dad was long dead, killed on a Porthcawl fun slide, while her mum was living with a torture murderer in prison. Her brother had died chasing a sheepdog into a ravine (a fate she'd always envied), leaving only an estranged grandma in Cardiff. She had no friends that I'd ever heard of: her schooldays in South Wales had been thunderously lonely, while her university years were a penitent trudge through a coastal town whose sole point of interest was a boglin museum. That left only me. And while I had no objection to attending, the exorbitant cost of train travel meant I'd likely miss the whole thing.

I stared at her lifeless face and tried to cry. I was sad, of course, but also strangely uplifted by her passing, as if waking from some disorientating dream. Maybe I was never destined to enjoy home ownership or week-long cava benders, and it was only my proximity to Sheena that'd enabled me to do so. Perhaps life would regain some semblance of normalcy now she'd carked it, enabling me to settle down and become a typist or gypsum plasterer. I resolved to get the necessary application forms tomorrow.

Rifling through her pockets for cigs, I tried to remember the good times we'd had. Dolefully I realised they were lost, now and forever, in a fog of alcohol and Thrushman's smoke. A part of me wished it *had* all been a dream, as my life would now forever be measured against the riches we'd once known, and I feared nothing would ever compare.

Having never before had any friends, I had no idea what to do when one died. Should I mummify her? With no bandages to hand I enacted the only gesture I believed she would've appreciated: I took a cig and wiggled it into her mouth, puckering her cold, dead lips around the filter. I lit it and watched it burn like a Paschal candle, blowing to keep it alight in the airless basement vacuum. I sat in silence as ash settled on her face, peppering her cheeks like cumin, and wondered if she'd enjoyed even a second of her miserable life. I concluded, contrary to the received wisdom of liars, that it was money and material possessions that'd brought her most happiness, and had in fact made her a better person. With a haunted fondness I recalled her face when our blackmail plot had succeeded: a gleeful, childlike wonder at the treasures awaiting those with such inclination to succeed.

Finally I rose and tramped up the stairs. I banged on the door in an effort to alert Muggins to the body in his cellar. I hoped he'd not mash her up and feed her to his customers' dogs, a legitimate possibility given his unswerving record of cruelty. 'Muggins!' I called, hammering at the door. 'Open the door. Sheena's dead.' I kept banging. Half an hour later it screeched open.

'Feeding time, friends.' said Muggins. He was sweating and brandishing a bucket of thistles. Had he been out foraging? 'Oh,' he said, meeting me face-to-face. 'What's the matter? Is there something wrong with the property?'

'Sheena's dead,' I said. 'Down there.'

'Oh Christ,' he said, stumbling down the steps. 'What happened?'

'I don't know,' I said. 'She must've had a heart attack.'

He knelt beside her and felt for a pulse. He shook her head and peeled open her eyelids, scouring for a spark of life. Eventually he relented, kissing her solemnly on the forehead. 'Goodbye dear friend,' he whispered, caressing her stringy old hair. 'Have a safe trip to heaven. If you see my wife up there, ask her what it's like to be free.'

'What happened to your wife?' I said, gobbling a thistle.

He grew sombre. 'She passed away,' he said, pulling a

binbag over Sheena's corpse. 'Her body gave up.'

'Crumbs.' I said, edging towards the door. He was still cradling Sheena's body as I dashed through the cafe and onto the street outside. I'd been compelled to run, as something told me that were I to be locked in again I'd soon find myself a drugged pawn on Wretchley's chess board. Despite my assertion that being kidnapped was a blessing in disguise, in this instance I felt it better to risk destitution rather than enmesh myself in a parliamentary torture ring. I'd be homeless but not without liberty.

I phoned an ambulance and waited on the street outside. There was murmuring from the customers as the paramedics arrived a short while later; bullish mithering from site workers with mouths full of sausage meat, rightly ignored as the medical personnel wheeled Sheena out and readied her for the incinerator. I approached them, wondering if I'd be able to nab a couple of night's sleep at the hospital, maybe in a sluice room or clinical waste bin.

'Who are you?' said the paramedic.

'I'm her business partner,' I said, trying to look tearful. 'Can I come to the hospital with you?'

He said something about forms but agreed I could travel with the body. We arrived at the hospital and they wheeled her out on a squeaky gurney, off to the rubbish composter or wherever the hell they disposed of bodies. I mooched in the reception area, gazing at laminated hygiene notices and gruesome posters of smokers' gums. Incidentally I was clucking for a Thrushman's but hadn't the money to buy any. Might I snaffle some from a surgeon's locker?

I was approached by a spry physician who gave me some documents to sign, as I'd been lumbered with next of kin duties. 'Have you got any cigs?' I said.

'No smoking in here, please.' she said.

'But it's what Sheena would've wanted,' I said, cleverly eliciting her sympathy. 'She *loved* cigs.'

'I'm sorry,' she said. 'You'll have to go to a toilet

cubicle if you want a cig. And you'll need to disable the smoke alarm beforehand.' She handed me a screwdriver. 'Jam this into the alarm casing. That should disable it long enough for ten or twelve cigs.'

'Thanks.' I said, begrudging of the fact I had to smoke in a cramped lavatory. Didn't she realise I was grieving?

'I'll sort you out a medical certificate,' she said. 'You'll then need to register the death.'

'How do I do that?' I said, miffed at the thought of even *more* admin. 'Can I do it online?'

'You'll need to make an appointment with the council,' she said. 'They'll issue a death certificate.'

I was resentful and daunted by the hundreds of certificates I was now required to obtain. I'd no doubt the council would take advantage of my grief and strong-arm me into a bureaucratic jobseeker's programme aimed at steering steelworkers towards suicide.

'Sorry for your loss,' she said, as if I'd merely mislaid a lunchbox. 'I'm sure she's in a better place now.'

Once ensconced in the toilet cubicle I jammed the screwdriver into the smoke alarm and gasped down twenty Thrushman's. The noxious, compost-brown smoke brought to mind Sheena's mottled gums and pale, ribboned lips; her dehydrated skin and rusty concertina wheeze. I had no idea what to do. My brain tumbled and rushed as I sought reason in the fathomless pits of death. Had Satan simply grown tired of waiting for her?

CHAPTER 25

As expected, the funeral was a damp, heartbreaking washout. Unable to afford the hilariously overpriced train ticket to South Wales, I'd convinced a long-haul lorry driver to take me, his only condition being that I massaged his bunions at rest stops. He dropped me on the outskirts of Swansea, where a further ten-mile walk brought me to Sheena's village, a cluster of wedged brick terraces and frosted-glass flag pubs. The chapel sat atop a nearby hillock, necessitating an uphill trudge that incensed my legs and left me choking with exhaustion.

The vicar muttered through a stunted, prosaic service before leading us to the sodden grave trench where Sheena's coffin would rot like a sunken slave ship. I stood beside her only living relative, a grandma from Cardiff who'd attended only under the condition she was provided a platter of chutneys. She was a pulpy old crone whose dentures clacked in her mouth like a bag of wet pebbles, and was convinced her family was cursed. 'Did you know my grandson died chasing a sheepdog?' she said.

'Sheena told me about that,' I said, trying valiantly to show sympathy. 'It's very sad.'

'I had the dog euthanized,' she said. 'I used its skin to make a shotgun case.'

Blimey, I thought.

'And my daughter's in prison,' she said, referring to Sheena's mother. 'She's got rat lungworm. From eating slugs.'

'How awful.' I said, quietly regretting the slugs I'd eaten for lunch earlier.

We stood by the graveside as the sky darkened and rain sprayed across our faces. Across the hillside I saw children rolling car tyres into the gorge below, their frenzied whoops lost in the braying crosswinds. The coffin was lowered into the mud and I considered leaping in after it. I had nowhere else to go and the wet earth looked like it might be council tax exempt. I daydreamed about cultivating a network of underground tunnels in which I could live, untroubled by skyrocketing utility costs, among the earthworms and ground beetles. The vicar finished his inattentive homily, murmuring some apocryphal verse about Sheena's place in the kingdom of heaven.

'That's rubbish,' said the grandma firmly. 'She's going straight to hell, that one. No question.'

Having fulfilled his obligations the vicar hurried off, presumably to evade molestation charges, and we tramped back down the hill.

'What are you going to do now?' she said, lighting a granny pipe. 'Are you staying in the village?'

'I'm not staying anywhere,' I said. 'I need to find a lorry driver to take me home.'

'Well I need a drink,' she said. 'Come on. There's a pub down the road. Let's drink to Sheena.'

I tried telling her I had no money but she waved me off dismissively. 'Don't worry about that,' she said. 'I've got plenty of money. Now Sheena's dead I might as well spend it.'

I slowed my pace. 'What do you mean?' I said. 'Now Sheena's dead?'

She drew her scarf in tight around her neck. 'You probably don't know this but I've not got long to live.' She reignited her pipe and hacked out a hot gust of smoke.

'They've given me six months. Apparently I've got a tumour so big it's grown teeth.'

'Teeth?' I said, thoroughly disgusted.

'Teeth,' she said. 'Little tiny teeth. Anyway, I had a heap of money left over from my witch burning days. When I died I'd planned on giving it all to Sheena.'

'How much money?' I said tremulously.

'A lot,' she said. 'Six, seven hundred thousand. I was a freelancer so I got paid a day rate, plus a commission for every witch I burnt.' Her voice lilted with a wistful melancholy. 'It was good work if you could get it.'

I was lagging behind her now, staring dumbly as I tried to grasp the ramifications of her words. 'B-but,' I stammered. 'Why didn't Sheena say anything about this?'

'She probably didn't know about it,' said the grandma. 'My solicitor kept sending her letters but we never heard back. Must've been lost in the post.'

With horror I recalled Sheena's practice of destroying every letter she received, terrified it'd be from a lettings agent or mercenary creditor.

'The solicitor said he'd take care of it all after I carked it. Said he didn't want to bother me with admin while I was trying to die.'

'Six months?' I said, evidently in a state of some shock. 'Sheena would've got the money in *six months?*'

'Probably earlier,' she said. 'I can't imagine I'll last that long. Apparently the tumour's also grown nails and tufts of hair.'

We descended the hill and I wanted to vomit for so many reasons.

~

We sat in the village pub drinking cider the landlord had brewed in a bathtub. It was rancid and cloudy as chicken stock, yet we tanked it with the fervour of jaded trauma surgeons. Sheena's grandma, as sick as she purported to be, seemed quite inappropriately sprightly. 'I can feel the curse lifting,' she said. 'I'm almost at peace.'

I tried to listen but was wholly distracted by the money. What would happen to it once the tumour finally killed her? Would she give it to me to buy back the apartment?

'Are you thinking about the money?' she said, rattling her dentures.

'Not at all,' I said, lying like an online influencer. 'I was thinking about Sheena.'

The grandma looked at me with a suspicious microexpression. 'What would she have done with it?' she said. 'Apart from drink herself to death?'

I took a mouthful of cider and pretended to procrastinate. 'She'd probably have bought our apartment back,' I said. 'She *adored* that place.'

'Well, we'll never know now,' she said, evidently clued into my ruse. 'She might've invested it. Or moved out here, bought a farm, settled down, who knows.'

'Yes, maybe.' I said, convinced Sheena would've done none of those things.

'What would *you* do with that kind of money?' she said.

My mouth opened but no words emerged. I'd always assumed my list of wants was exhaustive, yet the question left me oddly stumped. 'Buy a house I suppose.' I said.

'Nothing else?'

I pondered. What else was there?

'Don't you have any hobbies?' she said. 'Or would you want to travel?'

I shook my head. 'No.' I said. I'd long maintained that travelling anywhere was a senseless waste of money, especially given the ceaseless cost of renting.

'So you'd just buy a house and sit in it all day? Wouldn't you get bored?'

I explained that I'd never get bored as I'd not have to go to work, surely the most soul-destroying pursuit imaginable.

'Sounds lonely.' she said, causing me a strange, gnawing

discomfort. 'What about friends? Have you got any friends?'

I clarified that Sheena had been my only friend, joking that now she was dead I might as well kill myself.

'What's stopping you?' she said. 'Why don't you go and jump off a bridge?'

I explained how I wasn't *that* suicidal, but would happily welcome an accident if it was quick and painless. 'Like if a girder fell on my head.' I said.

We finished our drinks and stumbled out to the car. She slurred to me that drink driving was commonplace and perfectly harmless, and any resultant accidents were purely coincidental, usually caused by an old or faulty clutch. 'Bloody mechanics.' she mumbled.

'Yes they're awful.' I said, blithely assuming all garagemen were career criminals.

We drove through country lanes so dark I felt like a colonoscope snaking through an intestine. Eventually we hit the motorway, at which point she began to nod off, causing the car to veer into oncoming traffic.

'Wake up, old fool!' I cried, grabbing the wheel and steering us into a layby. We scraped against a crash barrier and ground to a halt.

'Where am I?' she said, fiddling with a hat pin.

'You fell asleep,' I said. 'We nearly crashed.'

'Bloody clutch,' she said. 'Maybe you'd better drive.'

Happily I was drunk enough not to be concerned with safety, springing into the driver's seat like a toddler with a machine gun.

'I might have another snooze,' she said. 'Wake me up when we get to Cardiff.'

I shunted onto the motorway and somehow drove us all the way to her house, stalling just twenty times and destroying only the gearbox.

~

212

I stayed in her spare room for a month, eating my weight in Willoughby jam and blood pudding, and left only once she'd bought me a leather knapsack and a first-class train ticket. I waved her goodbye on the platform, hoping my psychic manipulation had worked and that she'd bequeath me her entire fortune. I'd endured so much over the last year I felt it only right that a wealthy benefactor gift me an enormous heap of money. After all, there was no one else for her to leave it to, nor would she be able to spend it over the coming months. For what remaining outgoings did she have? Aside from oggies and a serviceable tombstone, there were precious few worldly expenses left for her to cover.

I sat on the train and stared as the countryside rushed by, vast and green and desolate. Sheep dotted the hills like dandruff and hay bales stood upright like Swiss roll. Soon the train would pull into Plugwood Central, where I'd alight with only the clothes on my back and a Tupperware full of crempog to my name. I had no home to go to, nor any friends to greet me. I'd lost everything and learnt nothing. I was insolvent. I was finished. I was free.

THE END

Printed in Great Britain
by Amazon